Sharp As A Razor

Sharp As A Razor

Book One
A Dying Wish

Chris Roy

NEW PULP PRESS

Published by New Pulp Press, LLC, 926 Truman Avenue, Key West, Florida 33040, USA.

For information contact:
Publisher@NewPulpPress.com

Printed in the United States of America
Visit us on the web at www.newpulppress.com

ISBN-13: 978-1945734069 (New Pulp Press)
ISBN-10: 194573406X

"Listen to me, boy! You can't out-punch this guy; you have to out-think him."

- Fred Williams

Sharp As A Razor

I. An Awkward Acquaintance

It's been a while since someone stuck a gun in my face. My line of work as a teenager had me looking at the wrong end of a pistol a total of six times. When I was eighteen I nearly killed a guy. Took his gun and beat his drug-addled head senseless with it. Drug related crimes on the Mississippi Coast haven't changed much in the nine years since.

This meth shooter in front of me is no different than the last idiot, a scared to death addict desperately seeking a mark in this quiet place of opportunity, hoping to stick me for a nice wad of cash he can poke into his scrawny arm.

I sighed with a sort of relief, trying unsuccessfully to suppress an eager smile. Held my hands up. I have been hoping, dreaming, for something like this to happen. Life has been BORING since I, myself, retired from crime. And the legit endeavors I've pursued in recent years are about as thrilling as watching two geriatrics drag race their electric scooters. This was the kind of danger I used to live for.

What happened to that guy?

He grew a vagina, my subconscious slapped me with. That nagging awareness has been too vocal for comfort lately.

"Give me your money!" the man shrieked at me, pistol waving, shaking two feet from my face. His shrunken features were pale, sweaty, and unshaven. Hair long and greasy, shinning grossly under the lights of the parking garage. His voice echoed off the concrete walls, roof, and the cars that filled nearly every slot. "You want to get shot? Give me your fucking money!"

I'm blessed with freaky-quick hands. Lethal weapons

that were far quicker than the eye, and enabled me to live in the world of crime for over a decade without carrying a gun. To my mind, the gun in my face was just another punch mitt for my left-hook to strike like a viper, a move that I've perfected in numerous gyms and dozens of boxing tournaments. I had absolute confidence I could hit and stun his hand before he could pull the trigger.

My upraised hands and shoulders relaxed a millisecond before my left hand darted at the side of the gun, fist tightening, punch smashing his fingers painfully into the steel, knocking the gun to my right, out of his hand. My other fist followed, a straight-right that drove into his fragile chin, two piece combo tapped out in less than a second. He must have been a career addict, body starved for calcium, because his jaw seemed to splinter into a dozen fractures, a crunch I felt and heard before resetting my stance, diving for the gun that clattered to the concrete.

He cried out, landed hard on his ass, hands going to his chin, cheeks. He squealed loudly, a scream that couldn't be voiced properly because of the inability to open his mouth.

I picked up the weapon and walked over to him. "Never stand that close to your mark," I said, tilting the gun upward. I opened the cylinder. Six .32 bullets fell into my palm. I pocketed them, wiped my prints off the gun and tossed into his lap. "Lame bitch. You deserve worse for being so stupid."

He whimpered in response.

I spun on a toe and marched off to the ramp leading to the next level up, feeling a supreme satisfaction that swelled my chest, arms, and Johnson.

Just sitting on the Hayabusa made me a king. The Suzuki was a '99 model, but had been rebuilt and customized so many times I've lost count. I put the key in the ignition between the handlebars, turned it. The headlight and taillight glowed brightly. Hit the starter button on the right hand grip. The 200hp race-spec engine ignited to life, powerful exhaust vibrating my entire body. My jeans, white tee and gray leather jacket buzzed. My arm hair stood up excitedly. The full-face helmet matched the bike's paint, white and gunmetal gray. I pulled it over my head and closed the face shield, secured the chin strap. The raw fuel smell in the air from the warming combustion chambers elated my chest as I backed the beastly machine out and tapped it into gear. Deafening snarls reverberated throughout the garage as I raced down the levels and onto Highway 90, leaving Pass Christian, heading to the interstate.

I had to hurry if I was going to be on time to meet my girl at our former trainer's house. I could picture her waiting in the yard, arms folded, foot tapping. I smiled broadly. She loved to have an excuse to fuss at me. Or smack me. I backed off the throttle, and decided to enjoy the cruise, helmet tucked behind the windscreen, relaxing on the top of the fuel tank, heading east in no hurry.

Exit 50 leads to Washington Avenue and downtown Ocean Springs. I went south towards the beach and turned into Eddy's driveway a few minutes later. My coach's home was practically a mansion. The colonial-style facade, white and blue, had several columns and a decked-out second-story balcony. As I drove up the long steep drive, I noticed the flowerbeds were empty, and the bushes weren't as trimmed as they looked from the street.

Guess it's hard to upkeep when you're dead, my subconscious told me. *Idiot.*

I growled away maudlin feelings threatening to weaken me. Thoughts of Eddy's murder are the only thing that's come close to making me shed tears since I was a teenager. When I was fourteen, my mother was killed during a police raid at a bikers' clubhouse. I haven't cried since. I have Rob to thank for that. He was an old outlaw Harley mechanic

3

that I hung with sometimes. I remember him grabbing my whiny ass, giving me a fearsome look, and declaring that my will is strengthened by Roxanne's death, a new sword pulled from a forge, emerging more mature, tempered and unbreakable. I loved the way that sounded, so it stuck with me.

As a kid the only father figure I had was Eddy. He opened the world of boxing for me. We lost touch after I met Pete and decided to make crime my career instead of professional boxing. I haven't seen Eddy in years, and I didn't feel as close to him as I used to. Still, *something* was going on in that supermax neuronal prison I keep my weaker emotions locked in.

Hmm. I simply did not care for this. FEELINGS are for the weak, the sheep, the lame.

The house was lit up, floodlights glowing around the yard. I glanced at my Tag Heuer, 9:36 p.m. Yeah, Blondie was fuming. I'm over half an hour late. *Good. A healthy argument, then awesome make up sex.*

I'll be sooo very sorry.

"Yes, I will," I murmured in anticipation, parking next to Blondie's truck, a '52 Ford. I killed the engine, extended the kickstand and doffed my helmet. With the helmet off I could hear a commotion that seemed to be coming from the backyard. I stilled my breathing, listening to the sounds of a ... fight.

It's a fight!

"Ah, hell!" I ran around the house and came upon a scene from my dreams. Blondie was in a ferocious battle with another girl, their long hair flying out around their heads, blonde vs. brunette, ripped arms and legs flexing explosively as they grunted feminine expulsions, fists flying. The floodlights played over them like special effects, bright rays that contrasted with the darkness surrounding them. I stood and watched, frozen and confused. The scene became a nightmare as I realized Blondie was way out of her league.

As a former world amateur champion, my girl has an advantage over most chicks brave enough to trade blows with her. However, this chick here was an animal, very obviously a professional fighter, strong and degrees faster than Blondie. I was debating whether or not to interfere. Blondie can't stand it when I save her, preferring to use her own very capable skills to take care of business. Fortunately (or unfortunately), the fight abruptly ended and made my mind up for me.

The enraged girl caught Blondie with an overhand-right that knocked her to the ground instantly. Blondie hit and crumpled, fight completely taken out of her, and I winced. She sprawled next to some geek whom I only just noticed, who was holding his stomach in pain, though outside the cones of light in the dark.

The girl spun in my direction, sensing a new threat, and my Johnson shrunk at the look she directed at me. An insane, feverish bloodlust had utterly consumed this girl. She was breathing like a rabid badger, growl-snarls that made her eyes lunatic wide. Nostrils flaring, veins standing up from her muscles like she was on every performance supplement known to man. She was about five-eight, one thirty-five, a couple inches shorter than Blondie, though ten pounds heavier. All high quality, highly trained muscle made her look like an Olympic Gold Medalist, showcased by her black tank top, running shorts, and compression sleeve covering her entire left arm.

She lunged at me, covering the twenty feet between us faster than any human I've ever seen, fists raised to bring the drama. I felt the stirrings of uncertainty before I raised my own fists and stepped into a comfortable stance. Something about this girl was familiar, though I had no time to ponder the possibilities before she attacked.

One-two-three-four! Her combo blazed at my head. I slapped down the first two punches, palms ringing from her power, swayed left, then back from the next two. Immediately I launched a counter four-piece combination. She caught and slipped, mirroring my moves.

Wait a minute ...

She pivoted, feinted a jab, jabbing hard right behind it. I read the move, leaning to the right and forward, throwing a jab that slid down her arm and, *POP!* Smashed into her cheek. Before I could follow up, a right-cross came out of nowhere and crashed into my ear, incredibly hard, nearly knocking me down. I stumbled and she jumped all over me, landing several shots before I could get out of her range. I circled around the crazed woman with a new respect, in awe.

You got to be kidding me. Where in the hell did she learn that? That was my move; take a jab to land a right-cross. It was like I was fighting, well, me.

She shuffled her feet, planted her back foot and lunged at me with combinations to my head and body, punctuating them with uppercuts that whistled millimeters from my chin. It was all I could do to keep her off me. I was so astonished by her speed, power, and skill that I couldn't rightly get in fight mode. I've never fought a woman before. I've sparred with chicks numerous times, but never thought I'd be fighting for my life against a girl that could scrap so viciously. She was literally trying to punch holes in me, her boxing ability a match to the very best I've been in the ring with.

I finally managed to land a right-hand. She didn't even blink, firing right back after my punch landed, nailing me with a right of her own. I shook it off, backpedaling. I sensed movement to my left and glanced over to see an enormous black dude standing over Blondie and the geek, a gun in his hand. He shouted to my opponent, "Boss! Move back! I got him!" He aimed carefully at me.

The girl couldn't, or wouldn't, accept his help. She was in complete submission to her killer instinct. Her demeanor said she just *had* to take me out. She was mad that I could box.

She darted inside my range and we began a slug fest, throwing as hard and as fast as we could, pummeling each other with hard shots, most caught by our arms.

I heard a brief scuffle and noticed peripherally that Blondie had recovered and somehow managed to take the gun from the giant. She told him, "No, you're wrong you big fucker. *I* got *you*". She waved the gun and he knelt down.

I fended off a blistering attack, pushed my opponent away from me, and Blondie limped over and stuck the gun in the girl-beast's face. "Get on the ground by your friends, you freaky bitch."

Before I could warn Blondie, the girl raised her hands and threw a lightning hook into Blondie's hand that was holding the gun. The weapon boomed a tongue of flame over their heads before flying fifteen feet away, slamming to the ground. Girl-beast followed with a right-hand bomb that would have broken Blondie's entire face if she hadn't turned aside as it hit, lessening the impact. Blondie scrambled away desperately and I ran over and tackled our enemy, rolling over on top of her, without intending to harm her any further, a daunting revelation striking me.

As I struggled to pin her down, I growled, "Stop! Wait a minute, you crazy motherfucker!" She grunted and strained, almost throwing me off. She was *so strong.* "We have the same trainer!" I yelled to get through her rage. "We *had* the same trainer. You were trained by Eddy, right?"

She blinked in sudden confusion, tension momentarily leaving her body. Right at that instant the giant black dude tried to take my head off as he speared me to the ground. The grass crammed unpleasantly into my mouth and eyes, the strong smell of earth forced into my nose. I thrashed and rolled onto my back, but the man was too heavy for me to budge with my stressed arms. Fighting the girl-beast had zapped my stamina. I caught a glimpse of Blondie crawling away, and realized she was heading towards the gun. The giant gave deep, growling rumbles as he tried to pin my hands. I resisted with everything I had left in me, quickly running out of gas.

The girl-beast was on her feet again, looking unsure of herself, as if the real her had returned and didn't know where she was. "Bobby!" she said. "Let him up." He obeyed instantly and a deep darkness was lifted as his mass moved from over me. I lay on my back, panting. The girl-beast's face appeared above mine, red and sweaty. "Tell your girl to stand down," she demanded.

I panted, nodded, held up a finger. I rolled over and saw Blondie had reached the gun and had a look on her that indicated she planned to murder first and ask questions later. She raised the weapon, face distorted in god-awful hatred. Tears mixed with dirt on swollen cheeks, and pointed the gun at the girl-beast.

I waved frantically. "Check yourself, Babe! It's a misunderstanding. She's one of Eddy's!"

She pulled the trigger ...

II. War Stories

Eddy's living room was spacious. The vaulted ceiling was twenty feet at its peak. Rough-hewn beams crossing in pleasing geometric patterns, all dark brown and white. Four large skylights showing the beautiful night sky. We sat on couches of the same colors in a semi-circle, around a huge low table and entertainment system in the center of the room. Stairs to the upper-level rooms behind us, kitchen and dining room to our right. Ice packs crinkled in the silence, three of the five people present nursing inflammation on various body parts. I was one of them. The girl-beast, Anastasia, as she was introduced, had landed more than one shot on the left side of my head. It throbbed intensely.

That's it. Back to the gym to practice defense ...

I grumbled to myself, plopped on the couch next to Blondie. She had her shoes off, legs curled under her, also nursing a swollen head with an ice pack. We glared at the others while they explained their reason for being here.

"First of all, I have to say I'm glad you can't shoot worth a damn," Anastasia told Blondie, who popped her eyes peevishly. Anastasia then turned her attention towards me. "I've known Eddy for years and he never mentioned either of you." She crossed her arms with a stubborn expression, seated on a love-seat with her boyfriend Julian, the geek that Blondie had jumped on thinking he was a burglar.

"Yeah, well, Eddy was disappointed that we didn't go pro," Blondie responded. "He didn't exactly approve of our career path." She tossed her long golden locks off her shoulder, shrugging as if it was no loss to her. But I knew better. I could see the pain it caused her to be reminded of it.

"What career did you choose?" Bobby rumbled, the big black dude that looked and moved like a Super Bowl MVP. He stood in front of the TV facing everyone, gargantuan arms folded across a pink bodybuilder tank top, with a look that suspected he already knew that answer to his query.

"Crime," I said, trying to keep from baring my canines. Most people get all uppity when learning of my past. They preach. Anastasia and her guys had Do Gooder written all over them. Even their names sounded law-abiding. So I didn't expect their response.

Julian smiled a little. Bobby pursed his lips and shrugged. Anastasia sighed heavily, *Not this again.* Her shoulders sagged, and I got the feeling she had long resigned to dealing with criminal types, or maybe had been involved in something illegal herself. She said, "Once, I would have looked down my nose at you." Another heavy sigh. "Are you still in that life?"

"Retired," Blondie said sharply, defensively, and couldn't keep a subtle hint of regret from her gorgeous face.

"Wait a minute," Julian said. He sat up straight. I was surprised that he was a couple inches taller than my six-one. "Razor and Blondie. *The* Razor and Blondie?"

"Umm?" Anastasia looked at Julian quizzically.

He looked at her. "These guys are legends in the darker realms of the Internet." He actually blushed with shame under her stare before looking back to us. Cleared his throat. "*Criminals.* You guys filmed your crimes and police chases and created an online show called *Criminals,* right?"

He looked like a kid meeting celebrities, and I couldn't help myself from smiling. I haven't enjoyed the feeling of infamy in some time. "Guilty," I said. Blondie gave a pretty smile of pride. I had to restrain my hand from pinching her boob.

"Whatever," Anastasia said unimpressed. I sensed she

was going to scold Julian later for his enthusiasm over our old show. Blondie looked daggers at her. Bobby was deep in thought. Anastasia continued, "We are getting off-subject. Why are you here?"

Blondie's body tensed, she unfolded her legs, and I grabbed her hand to calm her before she sparked another bout with the girl-beast. She hasn't acted this huffy in years. She must feel threatened by or competitive towards Anastasia for many reasons, and the girl-beast must feel the same about her. They were so different from each other it's unlikely they would ever get along. *Even if they were paid to,* I mused to myself.

I took a moment before answering, grimacing because I was unused to sharing personal information about myself with unknowns. I wasn't a Facebook kind of guy. But something told me I needed to connect with these people. Somehow I knew we would have met and connected strongly if I had gone pro and followed the law-abiding path. I felt like I could have just as easily had a life like Anastasia's, even though I had no idea what that entailed, and she could have easily had a life like mine. A simple choice of A instead of B could have seriously altered our paths. Maybe because her fighting skills were so much like my own that I felt this connection. I don't know. I sensed we were all here for a reason, yet another feeling that went against my norm. I didn't believe in destiny, fate, or karma. Things do happen for a reason, but the result is luck that you created with careful planning and hard work. Or the lack thereof. The rest was coincidence.

This has to be a plan of Eddy's. The thought came unbidden, my subconscious speaking up to let me know it's okay to reveal my hand, the explanation is rational.

"We are here because of this," I said taking a folded document from inside my jacket pocket. Anastasia's breath caught and she pulled an identical paper from her own pocket, white and gold trimmed stationery. I felt my eyebrows rise slightly.

"That old rascal," Bobby muttered with a faint smile.

"Of course. Eddy wanted you to meet them," Julian said to his girl. He ran his fingers through his spiked blonde hair, over his angular face. A thinking tic. He frowned in incomprehension. "Why now?"

She shook her head. "No idea. I didn't even know he had a will until I got this letter from his lawyer. All I knew was his brother was taking care of his house."

"What does your letter say?" I asked, eyes narrowed at her.

She stood, put the letter away and crossed her arms. The compression sleeve glimmered, skin tight against her muscles, showing the rips in her forearm and shoulder. The engineer in me wondered what it was made of. "It said to be here today," she said.

"That's all?"

She nodded, narrowed eyes daring me to dispute.

I shrugged. Mine said the same thing. This was getting boring. "Well, here we are, brought together for some kind of social intercourse. What now?"

"Intercourse?" Anastasia asked, eyebrow quirked.

"I always feel like I'm getting screwed in settings like this."

"Ah."

Blondie rolled her eyes. "A drink and a joint for me," she announced, standing and walking with a limp into the kitchen.

"I think I'll join you for a drink," Bobby told my girl, following her. "But I'll pass on the chronic. Makes me talk like Bubba on *Forrest Gump*." Anastasia looked at him querulously, biting her tongue, as if he was supposed to stay by her side because they were still not in agreement with us. She gave Blondie a suspicious look. Julian rubbed her shoulders and stroked her hair.

This was turning into an episode of *Big Brother*, a show I didn't particularly care for. I got up, deciding to do something about my boredom, following Blondie's example. Though I thought I needed something a tad more stimulating than a joint.

I went into the hall bathroom and shut the door, Lysol prickling my nose as I flicked on the light, the wall and floor tiles gleaming blue, green, and white. Towel racks as bare as the shower curtain rod. I turned to the sink and looked closely at the person staring into the mirror. *Intense* is how people describe me while I'm in earshot. I had to agree with that, and couldn't deny there being more derogatory descriptions. I've certainly been all kinds of motherfuckers with this face.

My dark, almost black hair was swept back over my head, longish in the front, shorter on the sides and back, thick and shiny, thanks to Blondie's TLC. My mustache was perfectly trimmed. Skin tan and smooth. Eyes green like burning gas, one scheme after another flashing under dark brows, the skin around them shaded from too little sleep and too much speed.

"I'll look like I'm wearing a ski mask after this," I muttered, smiling, taking a small Ziploc from inside my jacket. I could feel the weight of the straight razor before it slipped into my hand from the sheath snug against my lower back. The five-inch blade flashed chrome, silently opening from the gem-encrusted ancient silver handle, amethysts and rubies under my palm promising grip if I ever decided to use it for more than chopping narcotics.

As I tapped out some powder on the sink, the aroma of the cocaine filled my nose strongly, a piquing that told my body to buckle up. My eyes widened in concentration, my bowels stirred restlessly for a moment, hand blurring to line it up. I licked the blade, cleaned it with toilet tissue and sheathed it. Dug some bills from a pocket and rolled up a Benjamin like a straw, staining his fat little bald head with quality speed as I snorted a thick line up each nostril, snorting and groaning loudly.

The numbing, electrifying taste dripped into the back of my throat, and I cringed with the sickening pleasantness. "MMMahhh!" I roared, eyes darting, licking my lips. I cleaned up my mess, thinking I could deal with the women's drama now. I wouldn't be bored for a while.

I walked into the kitchen to find my girl chatting up Bobby, explaining how she took the gun from him earlier.

"Voodoo?" Bobby said skeptically, sitting on a bar stool, arms laying on an island counter. The kitchen made his huge frame look small, stainless steel appliances winking cleanly all around us, a dozen pots and pans hanging over the island.

"Voodoo that I do doo," Blondie sang with attitude, making her shoulders dance like a badass. She smoothed the front of her shirt, a purple and white blouse that showed off her fit tan stomach over Calvin Klein jeans. Black boots.

Bobby said, "That wasn't an answer."

"That's your opinion," she fired back, eyes squinting through pungent marijuana smoke. Bobby just shook his head and gave an exaggerated sigh, huge chest rumbling.

"Her voodoo mind tricks are nearly as frustrating as her fighting tricks," I said, smiling at them. She raised an eyebrow at me in warning. I left it at that before getting in further debt. I already owed her one for being late. A foot massage wouldn't cover that and talking smack about her in front of her new friend.

"Voodoo is from my ancestors," Bobby said. He looked at Blondie. "Never thought I'd see it whited-up. But you managed it." He laughed, deep voice quaking like a stack of woofers. "Voodoo that you do doo? I guess. The magic you pulled on me would make anybody a believer."

"Thanks," she said, then got up to get them more beers.

I snorted, earning a huge, wonderful drip. My eyes darted with ADD. Blondie sucked in a breath, looked at me sharply, while closing the fridge, and shook her head in disapproval. I shrugged *What the fuck?* at her, turned and walked into the hallway, humming *Cocaine* by Eric Clapton as loud as I could.

My mind couldn't focus on trivial issues. I craved something that would fully engage me. So I sought out the girl-beast to grill her about the science fiction-looking compression sleeve that, combined with her otherworldly physique, made her look like a cyborg.

She stood in the living room looking at boxing memorabilia on a wall. Pictures of marquees and fight posters from four continents covered one wall entirely. A montage of some of the sport's greatest moments. Eddy had been intrinsic to so many major fighters and events, and had a world-class collection to prove it.

Seeing all of it with Anastasia standing there suddenly made me realize why I've never met her until now – there are *so many* people Eddy worked with that I never knew. The wall of pictures slapped me with the fact that the girl-beast was just one of hundreds.

I looked at her eyes to determine what she was studying so intently. A framed picture of Eddy and a promoter named Silvio Vittorio, flanking a female fighter I remember from the 2000s. The Shocker. Eddy had trained her not long after leaving the amateurs to make real money in the pros.

A feeling of regret touched me briefly. *That could have been you in the photo*, my subconscious rubbed in my face. *You could have been a world champion, even more famous than her...*

I snorted deeply, and was rewarded with a zinging sensation that silenced the voice of my feelings. Anastasia glanced at me, but I ignored her, resumed studying the photo. The girl's hands were still wrapped, her face and hair sweaty, cheeks red and puffy. She had an inhuman glint in her eyes, wildly flying on all those intense chemicals that consume a gladiator during battle. This girl was on the level.

Recognition struck as if I had snorted a line through my dick. I managed to keep it from showing on my face. I looked at Anastasia and said with honor, "I fought the Shocker. That's the best thing that's happened to me in years."

A smile tugged the corner of her mouth, though she remained silent, still looking at the picture, as if waiting on me to complete the revelation.

I was missing something here. I looked back at the wall and suddenly remembered another, more recent picture I had seen of the Shocker. On *America's Most Wanted.* I laughed out loud, then told her, "You are a brave motherfucker. You still look like your mug shot." I held my fist out and she bumped it hard with her own, one boxer to another. I said, "So I take it you didn't enjoy the accommodations of Central Mississippi Correctional Facility."

She smiled. "I didn't belong in prison. My husband and I were innocent."

"What about the girl you killed in prison before you escaped?"

"Didn't do it," she replied, her smile gone.

I looked at her closely. "I believe you," I told her.

She continued staring at the picture, seeing through it with unfocused eyes. "Julian and I were Alan and Clarice back then. We were set up by drug traffickers and put in prison. Inside, I was forced into a fight ring. I went along with it, hoping I could use the money to finance my escape. The ring got busted the day before I was able to leave. I lost everything. The whole plan was nearly ruined, and wouldn't have worked without the help of my friend."

"Forced into a fight ring?" I sniffed. "That would be like forcing a fish to swim."

She didn't know whether to glare at me for being contrary or take it as a compliment and blush.

Normally I don't care for he-said, she-said drama. But this was an interesting discovery. She was a major fugitive, wanted by the federal government. She went on to tell me how Eddy died. He had helped her escape and was later shot while helping her rescue her son, who had been kidnapped by the traffickers. He took a bullet that was meant for her. She wiped tears from her eyes and I held back a grumble.

Don't walk away. You can tolerate this. It's worth it. It's a good story.

To refocus the conversation I said, "The traffickers were cops? Not surprising."

"Biloxi PD."

"They took your kid because you took six million cash from them. That was after you escaped?"

She nodded. "We wanted revenge."

"Taking a criminal's money is certainly the best way to pay them back," I said frowning, wondering what I would do if she had taken my stash. There was a lot more I wanted to know about her story, but she cut it short.

"Enough about me. Let's pick your brain now." She pointed to another wall and we walked over next to a trophy case full of Eddy's teenage achievements in boxing and football. Tall golden and silver awards filled five shelves, plaques on the mirrored back panel. On a shelf next to it were several framed news articles. The largest one, a walnut frame encasing an entire front page, headlined BATTLE AT THE FRONT BEACH! in bold. She said, "That was you and Eddy? I remember that."

"Oh yeah. I had forgotten about that. I used to have a framed copy just like it. Did Eddy tell you?"

"Some of it. You know how reticent he can be." She got a sour look. "Could be."

"*Omerta*. He followed the Italian code of silence."

"Don't I know it," she muttered. I smiled. Eddy had the same effect on me.

I was feeling loquacious. The drug had fully kicked in, promising great pleasure if I would only express myself, tell a feel-good story to reciprocate her sharing. I was beginning to like Anastasia for her personality as much as her accomplishments. It's not every day you run across the all-time greatest female boxer, who also happens to be on the FBI's Most Wanted list. And I like the fact that she's the obvious leader of a strong crew. Without a doubt she qualifies as a Badass in my book.

It's possible you're also warming to her because you no longer resent her for besting you, my subconscious jabbed at me.

I didn't argue. I felt privileged to have been punched by a legend.

She pointed her chin at the article. "Says here you and Coach assaulted seventeen football jocks."

I smirked. "I was able to hurt five or six. Got lucky. Eddy slapped down the rest."

"Sounds like fun," she said with that twinkle in her eyes, a mischievous predator lurking just beneath the surface. She was definitely on the level. Psycho.

I wonder if we're related.

She rolled a finger to prod me into giving details, and I began telling her about the incident that led to one of Ocean Springs' most spectacular stories.

~ ~ ~

Anger used to control my life on a daily basis. Hell, sometimes on an hour-to-hour basis. I didn't have much restraint over it back then, and even now I had to struggle to bite my tongue or halt my hands from slapping people I considered idiots. Which was almost everyone, unfortunately.

In '98 I trained my heart out for the Regional Championships. I made it to the final easily, and dominated some hillbilly for a clear victory. Only I was robbed. My hand wasn't raised. The judges favored my opponent because we were in his hometown. It was after that I discovered my anger issues made me a real danger to society.

As a way of dealing with the unfair pressures thrust upon my teenage-self, I developed my own therapy. My own twisted anger management: I would find a crowd of men – old, young, redneck, or gangster – and jump them. By myself. The more the merrier. The brutal ferocity I unleashed on them was soothing in a way that I couldn't possibly experience talking to some therapist about how this or that made me feel.

My trainer found out about my dynamic venting somehow, though I never knew how he did. I had never been caught. Turns out, he could relate to it. More, he *encouraged* it. It was the strangest thing. An adult telling me it was okay to hurt people to make myself feel better. But that was precisely what he did that day – after he made himself feel better, by giving the judges a scathing speech about screwing fighters out of a win because they weren't from Arkansas, didn't chew tobacco or fuck their cousins.

Eddy's insults had little effect, but his menacing glare seemed to scald the three judges' faces. He was pretty scary looking when he was in a *good* mood; he was absolutely terrifying right then. He continued, "You tea-baggers are a disgrace to amateur boxing. Especially *you.*" His deep voice boomed in the emptying building, thick finger directed at a pudgy balding man in a cheap brown suit. His two hundred and fifty pounds made the ring creak as he stalked back and forth in front of the judges, who still sat ringside, sorting papers on a table. Some fans overheard and shouted agreement. I stood outside the ring by the steps, angrily cutting off my hand wraps with Eddy's knife. He looked at me, then back to the judges, his anger growing. How could you give every round to that hobo?! He didn't win a single one! Do you know how much this boy has sacrificed to get here?" He pointed at me and demanded of them. "Look at me!" Three sets of eyes glanced up, then back down.

They didn't answer. I felt an awkward rage, the stirrings of rampage. I was impatient to leave. I couldn't vent here. I would go to jail for assaulting these clowns. They know they fucked me. *Well, I'm done with this shit. I lost. I was betrayed. They're not going to reverse the decision.*

They didn't understand that because of this loss people were going to look at me differently. Several sponsorships and endorsement deals just went into the same garbage can as my perfect record. They didn't understand that I would look at myself differently now. I believed that I could beat anybody in the ring. But as it turns out that bulletproof confidence was fallible, a bug under the shoe of a biased judge to be squashed at their whim. I've lost my first fight, and it felt like losing my virginity all over again. Only this this time it was a very BAD thing.

I wanted to curse these people out. I wanted to hurt them. *Why can't we just go?*

But Eddy wasn't done telling them what he thought of their corruption. He glanced at the crooks and stabbed his finger in my direction again. "I told this sixteen-year-old boy if he worked harder than everybody else, sacrificed more than anybody else, that he would win. He *did* work harder than anybody else, and he *did* win. Who are you three idiots to say otherwise, huh? Everyone saw what happened. The entire crowd booed your decision. I should come down there and slap all of you. You need to know what that feels like because that's what you've done to this kid:

slapped him in the face! "

That earned a few wary glances, but otherwise just made them speed up their paperwork. Experienced judges were used to disgruntled trainers, fans, or parents harrying them after controversial decisions. Eddy's outburst was nothing new, and would set no precedent.

Coach growled vehemently, obviously holding himself back from making good on his threats. He abruptly spun around and ducked under the ropes. Stomped down the steps. He walked past me with a red face and could only jerk his head for me to follow, tense with emotion.

In the parking lot people called out condolences, assuring us everyone knew who really won. We got into Eddy's car, a silver '74 Dodge Challenger, shut the doors. He started and revved the 440 Magnum, the big block bellowing a soothing roar. Gripped the steering wheel with both huge hands. His bulldog jaw stuck out in a smile, his French-Cajun features looking very Italian *Mafioso*. Chin beard and mustache dark and gleaming, eyes ominous under a thick brow. He looked over at me and suggested in a pleasant voice, "Let's find a nice crowd."

I smiled back. "A big one."

That night, around 2:00 a.m., we found ourselves on the beach in Ocean Springs, walking the length of the sea wall, looking for a large enough group of men to take our stress out on. It didn't take long. The beach was a favorite hangout for all groups of people, including the jocks we targeted and approached.

I recall that moment vividly. The sky was clear and showed the stars far out over the dark water. The sand glowed with dim moonlight. Cars and trucks lined the sea wall, doors open with interior lights showing couples kissing, drinking and grinding to the music. There must have been twenty football players in that crowd, all very familiar with free-weights, protein shakes, and any number of testosterone boosters.

Perfect. I love a challenge. I realized some part of me was screaming *suicide mission*, but I bumped Eddy's elbow instead of thinking about consequences, and he grunted an affirmative.

We walked right into the mix. At the time, I was five-ten and a ripped, highly trained one sixty-five. Eddy was five-eleven, two-fifty, a bear of a man with immense strength, and was capable of astonishing speed even though he was nearly half a century old. He had been a boxing trainer for over twenty years and that expertise made him a very dangerous person.

We ignored the scantily clad girls that looked at us curiously. I grabbed a beer from a cooler, walked over in the middle of several muscle heads that towered over me, and shook up the bottle. Twisted off the cap, held my thumb over the mouth and sprayed Bud Light in all directions, soaking as many people as I could. Girls squealed angrily as the beer wet their hair and makeup. Guys cursed and yelled at me over the music, a Cypress Hill song that wanted you to believe being insane in the membrane was a good thing.

I love it when the music fits the setting, don't you?

Eddy pushed through the men that encircled me, turned and faced them with his hands up placating. "Excuse me for a moment, fellas. Before we do this, the old man needs a stretch." He smiled and ignored the baffled looks he got, turned back to face me, and said, "Stretch my shoulders, boy." I pulled his arms behind his back and he grunted relief. "I'm too old to chase these youngsters. Just keep pushing them toward me, okay?"

"You got it, Old Man," I obliged, grinning psychotically, mind already racing with moves I planned to execute on the three guys behind me. My heart stepped up the pace, eagerness consuming me.

The loudest one in the crowd, a huge, angry dude in a

Dallas Cowboys hat, stepped closer and demanded to know, "What the hell is this? Who are you assholes?"

Eddy smiled at him. "We'll introduce ourselves in just a moment. Sorry for the delay. I'm getting old," he said apologetically, sounding very sincere. I let go of his shoulders. He sighed, held up his big fists as only veteran fighters can. He told the hulking jock, "My name is Gonnakickyourass," and drilled him with a left-hook that thunked an echo out across the sand, a monstrous blow that knocked the man sideways and to the ground violently, unconscious before he hit.

I spun around and threw a right-cross in one motion, back leg straightening to push my entire body in the direction of the punch, right fist a block of iron that hit my target's chin sickeningly. He dropped, out cold, knees and head thudding on the sea wall, and I pivoted to my left, reset shoulders, driving forward with a right-hand, left-hook to the body of the closest man to me, fists biting into his soft belly like cannon shots, his warm breath spraying me from the exploding pain as I stepped to his side and behind him. I shoved two more guys, trying to make room to dance with them, but they had the misfortune to walk into Eddy's scything arms, both going down instantly. I got outside the circle, darting back in to tag a guy in the head, knocking him to his knees. I never stopped moving forward, finishing him with a hook to the ear. He collapsed, smashing beer bottles beneath him. It was like shooting fish in a barrel. I couldn't believe how easily these guys were going down.

A tight-assed Asian chick popped up to my side, and my Johnson noticed her little boobies bouncing in a bikini top before she snarled like a thug and winged a full bottle of Corona at me. I ducked and it nailed some chick behind me, chipping her teeth. I laughed at her cry of anger then lambasted two, three more guys, punishing them with my assault. They went down, sand sticking to their bloody faces. I backed quickly out of the mix to let my shoulders recover and saw the Asian chick get punched by the girl with the broken tooth. I laughed again. I was having the time of my life.

"Insane in the membrane / insane, got no brain!" the music expressed in rhymes and thundering bass, fueling the chaos.

Eddy was out on the sand, halfway to the water, half surrounded by jocks, some limping, most angry, all too wary to run back inside his range again. My trainer looked like a warrior of ancient times, a combat expert teaching the next generation how fighting men were supposed to conduct themselves in hand-to-hand. I judged he was just about to break a sweat, his white Mopar T-shirt and warm-up pants moon bright. He moved with the kind of relaxed confidence that marks a fighter with a lot of fight in him.

I couldn't see his face clearly but knew he had a wicked smile. He feigned punches, causing his prey to jump. One guy yelled as if a quarterback had called hike and ran forward swinging wildly. He was silenced by a single uppercut.

"Come on, boys," Eddy said in disappointment, stepping over his victim. He shook his head sadly. "Do I need to tell y'all a story about how us old timers used to walk through snow uphill both ways? You guys fight like ninety-pound crack whores. Does anybody here have a set of balls? Raise your hand." Several curses erupted at that, and five riled steroid freaks moved in on him. "That's right. Come to Papa," he said, stepping in to meet them.

Peripherally I watched and heard Eddy's concussive blows demolish the athletes as I ducked and dodged four guys that chased me back and forth between them, loosely in a diamond pattern. I danced away until my shoulders and legs had recovered, then lunged in with a four-piece combination that simply overwhelmed one of my targets, a dark haired man about my size, though older. My punches hit him so hard and so fast he couldn't react to defend himself. His eye, nose and chin compressed, head snapped back, and he wailed a gurgling sound that always follows a severely broken nose, throat filling with blood.

I forgot all about him in an instant, relaxing to recover, lunging to my left with a feigned jab, jabbing hard right behind it at the next target's nose, dipping down and *forward*, twisting shoulders explosively to throw a straight-right into the soft area below the belly button, arresting his diaphragm. He forgot how to breathe and dropped, choking, gasping. One guy looked at his friends on the ground writhing in pain, looked at me, and took off running, leaping the sea wall, hurrying to his car.

His buddy followed a second later, carrying an injured man with him.

"Bitch," I said, appreciative of the Odds of war. The enemy had been routed. I turned around in a circle to survey the carnage, inhaling with deep satisfaction. The concrete area around the sea wall looked like it had been in the path of a tornado. Lawn chairs, beer bottles and wrecked coolers, clothes and random accessories were strewn all over the place, around and under cars, out into the street. Most of the girls had dropped their shit and ran.

I chortled merrily.

Screams resounded from down by the water. Half a dozen men, and two girls, were lying in the sand in various states of pain and consciousness between me and the water.

I hopped over the wall and followed the trail of knockout victims until a crowd of silhouettes materialized, white highlights of moon illuminating their aggressive faces, hair, muscle-bound shoulders. The football squad was determined to take down Eddy, a challenge they've rehearsed with their own coaches in a see-who-can-tackle-the-pro exercise. If Eddy had been just a ball player they would have tackled him by now. However, you can't tackle what you can't get your hands on, and Eddy's quick defense and mule kick punches were nearly impossible to get past.

The weak had been culled from the herd, the very strongest of the jocks the only ones still fighting. Eddy was in no hurry. He looked so calm and poised, fists held up almost casually. Then someone would bravely get inside his range and WHAM! Out of nowhere a single blow would crack. Another one bites the dust.

As I ran up on them, I realized the determination emanating from the athletes was part denial; they refused to believe they couldn't take down this one old man. Surely all of them together could get this geezer on the ground. I laughed because I've had the same frustrated anger on my face numerous times, while sparring with the same master that tormented them now. The pugilist guru could be infuriating because he could hit you so easily and block everything you throw at him. These guys had thrown everything they had and more at him, and have yet to land a clean blow. They were seeing red.

Knowing they couldn't hear my approach, the soft sand and loud wind masking my steps, I crossed the distance quickly. Eddy saw me, jerked his head up and grinned. I grinned back and shoved the two guys in front of me. Startled and off balance, their flailing forms stumbled forward like two logs tumbling down the chute of a wood chipper, BZZT! BZZT! ground into refuse where Eddy's whistling fists impacted, traumatizing skin, blood vessels, muscles and organs. Bones were fractured. They flopped around on the wet sand, hurt badly. The other guys, six left, circled away from me to avoid getting shoved into the meat grinder, who stepped over his latest work and moved in their direction.

Blue, red and yellow lights whipped back and forth across the sand, our faces and arms, accompanied by sirens blaring from the street. Our prey seemed to gain confidence now that the police were here, as if the danger had lessened because everyone was about to be arrested. They became cocky, but not stupid. With the clock running out of time and no significant points earned for their team, they left Eddy alone and turned towards me, the lesser threat, hoping to score something for the little pride they still possessed.

The sand made my mobility nearly non-existent. Without swift foot movement the odds of me getting hit increased. I didn't care. In a very disturbing way I looked forward to feeling a few hard punches. I still had some anger and stress built up, a ball of burning emotion sitting high in my stomach, feeding my will all the juice it could handle. I wasn't about to abort my mission for a few cops. I just *had* to get this out of my system. Stopping now would be like masturbation without the reward.

Two muscle heads bounded after me, sprinting for spear tackles, which told me that's the only training they've ever had, the only way their bodies know how to attack. The first one reached me and I waited until the last instant, his outstretched hands and snarling face *right there,* before pivoting to my right and throwing a right-uppercut under his arm, crunching my tightened fist into his chin and throat. A half-second later, my left-hook smacked solidly into his eye, closing it indefinitely. He landed on the sand screaming madly and a Mack truck hit me from the side, smashing me straight to the ground. The pain was voiced eloquently by my exploding breath and groan, sand silencing my open mouth. He held on, breathing hard, and I sensed he was either out of gas or surprised to have gotten me down, no further plan beyond the tackle, no further training or instinct.

I pushed my face out of the sand, blind, but happy that there was an idiot on my back instead of a fighter. Spat before inhaling, struggling with his weight. The sand burned my eyes, sucking the moisture away, replacing it with bits of clay and sea grass, a concoction I could taste and smell because the fucking shit had crammed into every hole in my face. My muscles had trouble working without air, and I couldn't break the hold the guy had on me. Wrestling and grappling wasn't my forte. I had to get him off and stand up to be effective at fighting.

I bit him. I don't mean a bite like a normal human bite. I lit his ass up like a big dog, sank my teeth into his arm like it was a warm, salty ham and snatched a plug of hairy, sweaty skin out. Blood squirted between my teeth, flooding my mouth. The acidic metal, warm redness triggered a frenzied response from my inner wolf, and my muscles swelled as the feeling of violent desire spread through the rest of me. Suddenly, I had retard strength, roaring primitive power that demanded to be channeled for one purpose: Destruction. My eyes flooded with tears. I could see again.

The jock felt lighter, a mere irritant to be swatted away, and I spun while throwing an elbow into his ear, continuing the movement to wrap my arm around his head in a headlock. The blow and lock were very unexpected, making him panic. I took advantage of the moment. Getting my feet under me I held the lock until I was sure I could spring away from him. I let go, jumped back, planted my back foot and immediately brought it forward with a heel strike that rammed into his collarbone, breaking it audibly. He screamed and thrashed around. I took a huge breath and felt a little closer to the Satisfaction line.

Flashlights traced beams of orange through the pulsing red, yellow, blue. Keys jangled loudly as several officers ran at us from the sea wall, screaming for everyone to get down. Eddy walked toward me from the water, dark silhouettes on the ground behind him, moon making him glow like a nightmarish specter.

The cops reached me, flashlights illuminating my face. They froze. One said, "Holy shit!" Then, "Don't move!" and pointed a gun at my head.

The blood was still warm on my face, sticky, spots on my shirt. My fists were held up in their direction, and I decided that was fairly stupid before realizing they must see a retard in truth, and I would be dead from a fusillade of bullets any second now.

"Razor! Get down, boy!" Eddy bellowed, jogging quickly, waving to divert their attention from me. He stopped, hands up, and two cops flanked him with aimed pistols. He got down.

I considered my options as the frightened policemen continued to yell at me. I could try to fight, but would likely take a bullet. I usually run from the cops. However, it's unlikely I'd make it ten feet before getting dropped by the giant Taser a policewoman just pointed at me, hands shaking.

I felt an emptiness in my gut where the ball of dense emotion had sat like a tank of nitro. I was certainly well past satisfied, with a reserve of satiety that should hold me for quite a while. I was pleasantly exhausted. A nap on a jail cell cot sounded terrific.

I'm good, I determined, shivering in fulfillment. I nearly shook my coat out. *No need to die today. And I'm not terribly eager to feel the bite of that Taser.* No fan of electricity am I. I got down.

We were cuffed and herded back to the sea wall. Two ambulances had arrived, adding more uniforms and blinding lights to the scene. People were being treated everywhere. Cops stared at me as we walked by. I became aware of the blood again, having to exercise great restraint in not licking it from around my lips. Stepped over the wall and got shoved into the back of a police car. They put Eddy in next to me. Shut the doors. The interior was cramped for me, so I know Eddy's bulk didn't like it, especially with his hands cuffed behind his back.

With no wind blasting me, I became more aware of myself. Both hands ached like a bitch, possibly fractured. My ribs were cutting up as well, pains I couldn't feel minutes ago as the aggressive emotions pumped me full of Fuck the World Indestructibility. I sighed, missing the feeling already, and wiped my mouth on my shoulder before I did something disgusting, like I was thinking a minute ago. *I need a joint in a bad way.*

I looked over at my trainer and new partner in crime and smiled, overall pleased with the outcome of our endeavor. "I feel much better," I told him.

He chuckled. "Me, too. But let's not do that again, okay kid? That felt *too* good, and I'm too old to start new habits."

I laughed, then cringed in pain. "Cool," I gasped.

We slept like the dead in the Ocean Springs jail, a small area of cells inside the police station off Dewey Avenue. The next morning we were told we had an initial appearance scheduled in court for 9:00 a.m. We were cuffed and led into a small courtroom that was filled to capacity, several people standing. All of the football jocks were there, some bandaged or in casts, several had parents with them. Pandemonium ensued when we entered, curses and demands for explanations, fingers and fists of angry parents thrown around emphatically. Shouts for quiet were ignored. Eddy and I were seated in front of the judge's bench, and I had to swivel around for fear of being assaulted from behind.

An air horn sounded, freezing everyone with its piercing blare.

"Quiet, I said!" the judge thundered, a late sixties gent in a black suit, black robe hastily thrown over it. He put the horn in a desk drawer. "Sit down and be quiet!"

The main entrance opened and Eddy's brother walked in. Everyone was stunned because Perry looked like Eddy's twin, huge and dark and dangerous in appearance. His glare made everyone think he intended to start trouble, but I could tell it was affected. Perry's a jovial dude.

He spotted us. I nodded, *What's up?* and he swaggered over to us. Stopped with hands on waist of his dark slacks. I admired his Cruisin' the Coast tee. He looked around at the victims, shaking his head. Everyone watched him, his presence eye-commanding. He looked at Eddy, at me, trying to hold a stern expression without laughing, and said in a scolding tone, "I thought I told the two of you: when there are seventeen of them, one of you has to sit out!"

Laughter erupted from several of the jocks' fathers. Their sons' faces turned scarlet. Perry barked a laugh that evaporated the spell he held on the court.

Perry took a folded newspaper from his back pocket and lay it on the table as he sat down between us. The judge began the proceeding, but I couldn't focus on his words. The headline of the Ocean Springs Record proclaimed BATTLE AT THE FRONT BEACH! and had a blown-up photo of the carnage. Police and EMT and hurt people were everywhere in the foreground, beach, water and sky dark in the back, moon bright. It was a beautiful picture. I decided to buy myself a copy and frame it.

"Did you really have someone's blood around your mouth?" Perry rumbled next to me. "Tell me they were exaggerating."

Eddy laughed loudly. The judge frowned at him. My grin felt like it would split my head in half.

"Would you like to share your humor, gentlemen?" the judge asked us, leaning forward with a scowl.

I looked up. "Not really."

His scowl deepened. I almost commented on how un-judge-like he looked. He shook his head and sighed. Looked around at the jocks and their parents. He said to the room, "I find this whole situation unbelievable. A star boxer and his trainer assault seventeen star football players on our very beach." He closed his eyes to show exasperation, but I could tell he secretly thought differently. As if he remembered some incident during his prime that held a special place in his heart. I could see he had been athletic once, and maybe knew what it felt like to take on impossible odds and win. There's no better feeling in the universe. He said, "I think I'll charge the lot of you and send you to the county jail."

Several people complained loudly.

"Quiet!" he screamed. "One more outburst and I *will* do that. You young men don't realize how fortunate you are no one was seriously injured." He ignored the looks of outrage from the men wearing casts. He looked at me, at Eddy. "You two will each pay two thousand dollars to the city, and you are ordered to compensate these young men and their parents for any hospital bills that resulted from your shenanigans."

He looked thoughtfully at the people that obviously wanted to protest. Looked back at us. "Because of your status in our community and the good you have done for our youth through boxing programs, I am lenient. I won't be next time. You understand?"

"Yes, sir," Eddy and I said together, suppressing grins.

"Good. Dismissed! All of you get the fuck out of my courtroom."

"Did he really say 'fuck'?" Bobby asked me, sitting on a couch behind me and Anastasia, Blondie and Julian on either side of him. They shared a bowl of popcorn, and from the looks of it had been there a while. The bowl was nearly empty, empty beer bottles on the table between us. My dry mouth told me I had gotten carried away, talking for a long time. *How long? Damn cocaine trance...*

Anastasia looked at me quizzically. I realized she wanted me to answer Bobby's question.

"Yes. He said 'fuck'." I took a breath. Snorted. *I need to get re-keyed.* I talked away my buzz.

Bluh!

"Damn good story, Babe," Blondie said, crunching popcorn.

"I'd buy a ticket," Bobby agreed and tossed a kernel in the air. Blondie's arm flickered deftly, catching it right before it hit his open lips. She crunched it loudly, looking at him with her Shall We Duel? look. He chuckled in high spirits.

"I thought you said you had forgotten about that," Anastasia said, smirking. "I doubt any story that has Coach in it is boring. All mine are unforgettable."

"Can't wait to hear more of yours," I said as a courtesy. She smiled. I turned around and muttered, "Big Brother" before maneuvering around her. I've had enough social intercourse for now. I went into the hallway, intending on revisiting the launch pad, and remembered something.

Shaking my head, I spun back, stuck my head around the corner and glared at my girl. She lounged on the couch like a supermodel. She noticed me and I amped up my glare. I said, "Popcorn? Really, Babe? I'll twist your blonde pubbies for that."

She squawked in a very satisfying manner, and just like that I was out of debt. No foot massage for her. Bobby and Julian hooted laughter. Anastasia gave me a look that said, *Why I never!*

Blondie smiled sensuously to acknowledge my one-up, gave a slow, foxy wink that promised unspeakable pleasures and tapped her nose, bright green fingernails gleaming. My Johnson took note. I waved for her to follow me to the bathroom.

III. A Dying Wish

"Before I tell you, I want you to call me Shocker," Anastasia said when I asked her what the hell that thing on her arm was.

"And I'm Ace," Julian said, smiling at me and Blondie. He and Shocker sat on the loveseat facing us. Bobby kicked back in a recliner with a Michelob and listened, all of them pretending they hadn't heard my girl cry out in orgasm minutes ago. Blondie's face was still flushed, an interesting shade that differed slightly from Shocker's prudish embarrassment coloring her cheeks.

I looked at Shocker and Ace, shaking my head. "Good. Now my Lame Detector won't go off every time I hear your names." I blew out an amused breath. "Anastasia and Julian. Geez."

Blondie and Big Swoll laughed, but Shocker and her guy didn't think it was funny. Hey, they shouldn't have chosen names that invited ridicule. If I knew them a little better, I'd roast their asses.

"Murderize," Shocker blurted.

"Huh?" I turned my head to the side.

"Sometimes I hear voices. They like to create words for the moment. The fight junkie in there just suggested 'murderize.'" She smiled, showing too many teeth. "I like it."

"Me too." I returned her canine smile and her entire body flexed, looking every inch the freaky-built athlete, her so-called inner fight junkie straining to come out. My head throbbed in warning, perhaps to remind me of her ability to make murderize a real word. Blondie unconsciously gripped my arm, and I thought, *Okay. I'll have to check my candor around her. Until I brush up on my defense, anyway...*

"The compression sleeve is a recent creation of my husband's," she said after taking several calming breaths. She inclined her head towards Ace, who adopted a proud squint at her words.

"Uh," the geek said, getting his thoughts together. He was definitely of the intelligence elite. He knew most people couldn't follow his train-of-thought, so he simplified his prose for us. "It's electroactive polymers."

Blondie jerked up straight, staring at him in disbelief. "You work in materials?" she asked, referring to the engineering field.

Now it was his turn to stare in disbelief. *Maybe I don't have to dumb down my explanations*, his raised brows expressed. He looked pleased and confused.

Blondie chortled, said, "You actually figured out how to control an electrical response from polymers? I thought that was only theoretical."

"Technically it is. This prototype is unknown to the scientific community."

"And we have no plans to advertise," Shocker added, watching Blondie, baffled that this girly-girl was knowledgeable on the subject.

"Understandable," I said. Everyone nodded.

Ace went on, speaking excitedly. "The polymers bend and stretch just like muscles. The inner layer has sensors that intuit muscle fiber movement, telling the material how to contract or stretch to assist. The sleeve adds substantial speed and power to her punches."

"Power source?" Blondie quizzed, standing and walking to study the sleeve intently. It looked like liquid metal, black-silver, reflective. A small ribbon containing wires came out of the top of the sleeve at the shoulder and plugged into her tank top.

"Surprisingly, it doesn't require much voltage. So I

designed this tank top that converts core body heat into direct current. It powers the sleeve. The hotter she gets, the better it works."

I chose to ignore that straight line, humor the geek didn't seem to understand. Everyone but him snickered. I looked at Shocker's black tank, which was tight against her torso but showed no outward appearance of being comprised of anything special. It looked like a thick, expensive shirt you'd see on a rack at Macy's.

Blondie sat next to me again. Looked at Ace. "Power Felt?"

He nodded, impressed. He must now realize she was a student of engineering. With her Giselle-like looks she fools everyone. He looked at her hands, perfect long fingers that were unlikely innovators, appearing more suited to creating hair styles than mechanical or electronic inventions. He looked back to her expectant face. "Carbon nanotube based fabric. It creates a voltage from a difference in temperature between the skin and the outer layer of the shirt. Heat energy on one side of the material sets electrons in motion. They slow down and accumulate on the cooler side, generating a voltage."

"You could probably charge a cell phone or run a flashlight with it, huh?" Blondie ventured, tapping a finger on her bottom lip.

"Sure. Maybe power a laptop. All sorts of accessories."

"Why only one sleeve?" I asked.

Shocker looked at me. "I was shot in the left shoulder while rescuing my son."

"Ouch," I sympathized. "Bullets are a bitch."

"For sure." She rubbed her shoulder. "Thirty-ought-six. Shattered my humerus." Ace squeezed her other shoulder and she gave him an appreciative smile. She told us, "Ace thinks the titanium in my arm is boss. Don't you, sweetie?" She stroked his hair.

"Yes dear," he murmured like a dork.

"*Big Brother*," I grumbled in reflex, though for some reason didn't quite feel the disgust for their drama that I felt earlier.

What are these people doing to me? I care nothing for them, I told myself, not believing it.

I snorted loudly, and like a yawn that's contagious, Blondie sniffed next to me. I looked at her. She smiled, teeth bright and perfect. Pert nose turned up slightly at the tip. She wore only lip gloss today, no other make-up. She didn't need it. Her face, even tweaked out on coke and just-fucked-flushed from our bathroom snort-and-hump, would be the envy of any girl if it were on the cover of a magazine. I looked down at her blouse, perfect round boobies swelling out of a black lacy bra. I hung my tongue out, panting, leering at her chest like a perv at a strip club. "Babe, I like how your boobies are presented today. It's like they are making a speech, informing the haters that there's a new standard to hate, and demanding double attention from all who admire the aesthetics of a quality bosom."

She rolled her eyes, lips twisted to hold in a smile. "Raz, the score is even. We settled that on the sink. Stop trying to start more shit just so we can fuss then fuck again."

"Worth a try," I grinned. She smacked me for my effort.

"Uh," Ace uttered, looking like he was going to ask if we needed privacy.

"Whoa," Bobby said. "You guys are crazy even for white folks."

"Yeah. They should have their own reality show," Shocker said sarcastically, suddenly impatient.

"We did," Blondie shot back.

"You should watch it," I suggested, ignoring her attitude.

Shocker glared at me. I gave an exaggerated glare back and she laughed. She looked around at everyone. "I don't know about you people, but being here has made me emotional. All I want to do is go home to my kids."

"You have kids?" I asked. That was unexpected.

"Two. A boy and a girl."

Blondie squirmed. I grimaced, recalling our recent conversation about our future and the possibility of having kids. She wanted one. I wasn't ready. She didn't exactly demand that I play her or trade her, though it was close. Thankfully, I've been able to distract her with sex toys and drugs (Yes, I realize this is wrong. Fuck you for pointing it out. I'm just not ready to commit yet, okay?).

I could tell my girl wanted to grill Shocker for details on her rug rats, but was reluctant to engage her in girl-talk. Worked great for me. I was about to put on some music and suggest everyone get up and shake their ass, guzzle some more beer, when Eddy's brother walked in the front door.

"Good. You're all here," Perry said, closing the door. He walked in, stopped next to Shocker and Ace. He was six feet, nearly three hundred pounds, dark hair short on a massive head, chin beard, enormous arms holding several bags of groceries, which crinkled against Levi's jeans and a simple green shirt advertising the Beau Rivage Casino. He was probably the finest cook I've ever known, his under bitten smile and dark, twinkling eyes excited about creating some gastronomic extravagance that weighed heavily in the Winn Dixie sacks. He took his time scrutinizing the five of us, his presence as eye-commanding as ever, once again bringing to mind that day in court that made local history. Smiling in genuine cheer, he told us, "If you want to eat, get your asses outside and unload the groceries," then walked into the kitchen, knowing we would do as he bid.

With a stomach full of cocaine drip I wasn't hungry at all, but knew I should eat something. I usually eat six small meals a day, a regimen that keeps my metabolism soaring, burning fat and processing nutrients much more efficiently than a traditional three meals-per schedule would. It was a job to eat while flying on speed, but necessary. I was thankful that Perry offered to break bread. It's been too long since he, Eddy and myself sat in this very house gorging on ridiculous amounts of food. I couldn't forget the quality of Perry's and Eddy's cooking if I had Alzheimer's. I ate here for years as a teenager.

"Chow time, Babe," I said, slapping Blondie's thigh, standing quickly to avoid her counter. Her hook blurred inches from my stomach, thumping hard into the back of the couch. She squawked at the miss. "Ha," I said with malicious delight, dancing away as she flipped me off. I turned, heading outside to grab some grocery bags. Everyone followed. The load from Perry's truck, a tricked '49 GMC that nearly glowed in the dark from the orange paint, emptied in minutes.

With a satisfied chuff after the groceries were laid out on the island counter, Perry scrubbed his hands at the sink and moved around the kitchen like a mentor on *Master Chef*. He picked through cabinets and drawers, grabbing various pans, utensils and in minutes the mélange of heating sauces, marinating meats and chopped fresh vegetables intoxicated us.

Music began jamming in the living room. *My Girl* by the Temptations accompanied by Bobby's snapping fingers. They sounded like .22 rifle cracks. He stepped around like the legendary band members did on stage, swinging arms, tilting shoulders, humming, fresh beer in hand. Blondie giggled, watching him for several minutes before joining in his harmonizing hum and dance.

I looked back into the kitchen. Ace and Shocker chatted while washing lettuce and tomatoes, handing them to Perry, who chopped them for salads on a huge wooden cutting board mounted on the island counter, blade blurring *tat-tat-tat-tat* in his tremendous hand.

I was not used to what was going on here, beginning to feel extremely uncomfortable. The only time I ate with a group of people was at restaurants, and they were all complete strangers, not people I liked.

Thought you didn't like these people, my subconscious mocked.

"Sorry bastard," I grumbled at myself and the situation. I didn't like being outside my comfort zone. It wasn't just the eating together. It was the camaraderie, the friendly-feeling-and-goodwill bullshit. I prefer to spend my life in the company of my bitch and my bike. I like parties and clubbing on occasion – who doesn't like dancing, drugs, and a herd of marks – but this was something entirely different. There was no percentage for participating in this. It felt high-maintenance, filled with drama, and, the worst part, these people were not expendable witnesses.

"But I can't ditch them now," I sighed.

I looked around at my new acquaintances, reluctantly submitting to the alien feeling elating my core. *Ugh. Feelings.* Then, relenting the last of my cynicism, *At least they aren't posting every minute of their lives on Twitter.*

Perry caught a break while waiting on things to cook. He waved to get everyone's attention and announced, "I have a surprise for everybody. Including myself, come to think of it." He chuckled. "I haven't seen it either."

Everyone murmured in pleasant surprise, crowding around Perry as he turned on the TV in the living room, a fifty-five inch Sony plasma screen. He loaded a DVD into the side of it, used the remote to start the video. Suddenly my trainer's enormous head filled the screen, ten-times life size. It was fairly disturbing. He looked healthy, slightly older than the last time we spoke twelve years ago, though basically the same dynamic bulldog with gorilla strength that I used to love like a father. Seeing his face on video made me miss him more than the obituary photo had.

You know that feeling? Shitty.

Eddy smiled, jaw kicked out as if to say, *You ready for this?* He looked straight ahead, seeming to know Perry would be standing in the middle, having started the video and stepped straight back. "Thanks for handling this, Perry. If things work out this crew may become part of your life. God knows they need you."

Eyebrows around the room rose at that, lips pursed or frowning. It was a bombshell. The idea of us becoming familial hadn't been thought of, much less voiced. And wouldn't have. Eddy, always putting people on the spot, just slapped all of us with planet crushing pressure. It's actually hard to make six people uneasy with a couple of sentences. Eddy did it as if reiterating something he had studied in the *Book of Destiny,* an oracle only accessible to those that are as worldly and knowledgeable about humanity as my trainer.

He resumed. "No pressure, or anything." Another smartass grin, then he addressed the girl-beast. "Clarice. The Shocker. You are my most special achievement. My legacy as a trainer is extraordinary because of what you accomplished in the ring. My pride as a mentor is extraordinary because of what you've accomplished as a woman, a wife and a mother. A business owner."

He went quiet, groping for words. Shocker sniffled, tears streaming down her cheeks. Everyone grew more uncomfortable. I felt like I wasn't supposed to hear all this endearment BS, and wasn't exactly thrilled to be part of it. I snorted, shifting foot-to-foot.

Eddy looked to his left, right at me, and barked, "Razor! Boy you need your butt beat for so many reasons." Heavy sigh. "But regardless of all the STUPID in your life you're still a good kid. You made the Old Man proud countless times. We had a good run in the amateurs, didn't we? Lots of memories that I cherished. I hope your kids and protégés make you as happy – and as frustrated – as you made me. You worked hard, son." He smiled, then shadowboxed a few combinations.

I grinned back until I noticed Blondie looking at me pointedly. She quirked a brow, inclined her head at the TV, hint-hinting, and it dawned on me she took Eddy's mentioning of kids to heart. Jolted as if stuck with an ice pick, my smile vanished. It was hard not to glare and curse at Eddy's virtual presence. *That old bastard!*

"You were a sore spot in my life," he told me. "But Pete Eagleclaw taught you well. Turned you into the criminal mastermind you are today." His jaw kicked to the side, and I remembered the expression as being the one he wore for exaggerating or sarcasm. "The infamous hustler known by every crime family and street gang from Florida to Texas."

I groaned, ignoring the odd looks I got. *That old bastard!*

Eddy turned serious. "Even though I got away from that style of life two decades ago, the crook in me grew fond of your achievements in the underground. When I heard you quit I didn't believe it. I wanted to, but... couldn't. I just knew you were going to end up in the joint. For once I was glad to be wrong." He gave a sigh-hum of satisfaction, a wan smile.

I glanced at the others, feeling embarrassed. No one has ever talked to me like that. Eddy sounded like some soap opera father gushing after reuniting with his estranged son. My system wasn't wired to process this shit. My fists balled, and I swear I would have KO'd anybody that tried to hug me right then.

I growled, tried to relax. Blondie wisely kept a neutral expression.

Eddy looked to my side, at Blondie, his uncanny knowing of our positions unnerving. The man was dead, yet here he was talking to us like we were really standing in front of him. "And my beautiful Blondie. I had high hopes for you after you won the World Championships. With your jab and knockout looks you could have been a celebrity among celebrities." He shook his head wistfully. "You were another disappointment though. At first I thought your love for Razor blinded you, that you were under his influence. But I changed that view. It was *I* who was blinded; your appearance and sweetheart personality has probably fooled countless old geezers like me, huh? Who'd of thought you were a natural born crook. I must apologize for trying to convince you to leave Razor."

"He told you to leave me?!" I sputtered to my girl. I couldn't keep the shock off my face. She had never mentioned it.

She waved me off, wiping tears from her big glistening eyes. The shock registered full-tilt upon seeing this. She *never* cried. Still looking at Eddy she said, "He thought I would end up in prison if I stayed with you."

Everyone but her gave me suspicious looks. I scowled *Mind your own fucking business* at them, pointed at the TV.

Eddy said, "Now that I've told my children how I feel, all hard feelings aside, we can get to the meat of this sandwich." He cleared his throat of emotion, clasped his hands in front. All we could see was his head, his shoulders in his U.S.A. Boxing jacket, and a white wall behind him. "A couple years ago I began working on a project with far-reaching implications. It became dangerous, and I knew there was a chance I would be killed. Hence the will and this pleasant video." He gave a lopsided smile, turned serious again. "This job needs to be done. I can't think of a better crew to punch this out than you guys. I could handle it solo for the most part, gathering intel and pulling strings here and there. But I'm dead now. Forget about it." He shrugged. "I felt confident my kids would pick up where I left off. All of you are well-off to the point monetary gain holds little interest to you. You are all retired from your various professions, and likely bored stupid. You are far too young to travel the country in an RV or play out the rest of your days on a golf course." He made a sound of disgust at that thought. "So what better inheritance could I possibly give you? I asked myself. A chance to make a difference in the world. You can do that with this job."

"What the hell is the job, Coach?" Shocker shouted, frustrated in a way I could relate to. I smirked.

Eddy pointed at her. "I knew you'd ask that." He laughed. I looked at Perry, briefly thinking this was some kind of prank, that Eddy was alive, in the next room screwing with us. My conspiracy theory faded. Eddy said, "Serious business now. The organized crime on our Coast is rarely anything major, but it affects nearly everyone, if only indirectly. The problem is, it's becoming unorganized. And that means serious trouble for everyone from politicians to soccer moms.

"The Vietnamese street gangs are the culprit, encroaching on everyone's territory, taking over rackets and squandering them carelessly. They are making it hard for the old Viet Mafia to keep the peace. It's Bad Business," he growled, then looked at me. "As the Alpha criminal in this group I'm sure you're wondering why I give a rat's furry ass about the Vietnamese. The answer is complicated. I care about my home, and that includes all the good and bad of it. The entire economy of the Coast. Think about how many businesses the Viet Mafia has their clever chopsticks in. It's substantial. If they lose control of that empire to these saggy pants, water-head thugs, it will collapse, taking everyone connected down with them. Hundreds of jobs will be lost. Maybe thousands. Kids will be homeless. People will be killed. The ramifications are impossible to calculate."

"I could calculate it," Ace muttered. Shocker elbowed

him into silence, as if he were revealing a secret. Bobby nodded at him with a Damn Right frown. Blondie and I looked at them curiously, back at the TV.

"There's quite a lot more to this story. The bottom line is, the old Viet Mafia knows how to take care of business. Sure, they run dope, work prostitutes, launder money and evade taxes. All the goodies. But they do it *economically*. Everyone benefits. These new kids don't have a clue. And, to add gas to the fire, they are breaking truces with the black gangs. Banging, doing drive-by's and nonsense like that. They have no respect for what's left of the Dixie Mafia or the Italians, and are on the verge of outright war with La Familia, the latest crime family to claim a chunk of our turf." His sullen grimace showed what he felt about that.

"El Maestro's people?" Shocker said uneasily. Ace and Bobby both looked like deer caught in headlights. Shocker glanced at me. "I'd hate to be in the middle of a war with them."

"You know El Maestro?" I queried. This girl really gets around. I wasn't really surprised she knew the leader of a major drug cartel. She boxed professionally all over Mexico, and a dozen other countries run by organized crime.

"Unfortunately," she grumbled.

"The Two-Eleven are the main instigators," Eddy informed us. "They have allies of similar brands. All of them lack brains, though they have the muscle and audacity to cause serious damage, possibly even take over the Mafia. We can't allow that to happen."

Eddy paused to consider a conclusion to his dying wish. I pondered how any of this could affect me, my bitch or my bike, and if I even cared. With stunning clarity I realized that I *did* care. This was my home. My stomping grounds. The thought of it becoming more dangerous bothered me not in the least – that was perversely exciting. Though I knew in the long run it would be too much to deal with. We had more than enough winos, crackheads and idiots around already. And I didn't want to see any kids suffering, hungry or traumatized because their parents lost their jobs or homes or were scuffed by some gangster with an AK and no I.Q.

You wouldn't want to raise your *kids in a place like that, right?* my subconscious threw in my face.

Goosed, I couldn't keep my expression neutral. Blondie looked at me, similar thoughts running through her pretty head. We stared into each other's eyes, no words necessary, our minds churning the same gears. She saw that I was worried, a rarity for me, and knew it wasn't apprehension over thugs with guns. She deduced that my concern was about our future, and everything that entailed. She turned and hugged me, assuming far too much for my comfort. My fists balled autonomously. I wanted to curse her for the pressure gnawing at my bones. I wanted to spank her. But in the end I just sighed acceptance and squeezed back.

She smells so good, my Johnson noted.

We let go and turned back to the TV. Shocker and Ace were holding hands. Eddy had a devious look, a master in front of a camera, showing off his years of experience of being filmed at boxing promotions. In a formal tone he said, "Your mission, should you choose to accept it, is to neutralize the Two-Eleven, their allies, and restore the old Viet Mafia to power. As always," he chuckled, "if you are apprehended, I will deny any association to you or the mission. This message will self-destruct in five seconds." He stepped closer to the camera and suddenly punched it.

The screen went black and we all laughed. Except Shocker. She darted forward, hit OPEN on the DVD player, waited impatiently for the tray to eject, and snatched the smoldering disc out, shouts of surprise echoing off the tall ceiling as she frisbeed it into the hallway. It landed on the tiles, barely missing an expensive rug, smoking, burnt plastic filling the air. The cordite in the disc would have ignited the carpet under our feet. The girl was a quick thinker. My esteem for the legend rose a little further.

She sighed, wiped her hands on her shorts, turned to look at us. Shrugged. "Coach never left behind any incriminating evidence."

Blondie and I shared a surprised look. "Pete Eagleclaw," we said together. Our engineering mentor made that DVD for Eddy.

What the hell?

IV. Team's First Job

It was entirely too much food. The table sat twelve in the spacious dining room, white floor shining, dimly reflecting the dark green walls, plain except for a seascape painting hanging behind Perry at the head of the table. The six of us were spaced out evenly, Bobby facing Perry at the other end, Blondie and I facing the girl-beast and geek. 70s rock played from the living room, the guitar riffs making my foot tap and head nod without thought. Pans and bowls mounded with steaming delights were picked over with gusto by a dozen hungry hands. Crab claws and asparagus were passed politely, melted butter summoning much appreciated saliva to my coke-cotton mouth. We munched chopped rib eye steak in pita wraps, crunchy fixings of salad and strong cheddar falling to my plate after every bite. I wolfed it down. The food overpowered the drug, and I began to feel privileged for being here.

I sipped a tall glass of sweet tea, unable to keep from comparing the women's eating habits. Blondie took her time between bites, talking and laughing with Perry, Bobby, and would eat maybe two-thirds of her plate. The girl-beast was all business, no talk, having eaten her steak wrap as quickly as I had, eyeing another as she cut asparagus into bite-size pieces. Perry and Bobby, both giants, were able to talk while consuming inordinate portions.

Perry stood and excused himself, returning a moment later with a stack of manila folders, important looking files an inch thick. I realized what they must be right as he said, "Files on Eddy's project." He flipped through one at random. "Looks like photos of individuals, homes and businesses. Lots of detailed notes. This was a year of work, at least."

Shocker and I reached for them at the same time. We grabbed an end of the stack and pulled, neither willing to let go.

Perry grinned, swatted at our hands. "I'll hold these for now, until you figure out an arrangement."

I looked at her, trying to project reason. "It's unlikely anyone in this room knows more about the Viet underground than I do."

Blondie folded her arms, looked at Shocker, lips pursed in a *Let my man run this shit* attitude. Bobby and Ace seemed indecisive, evidently used to following the girl-beast, though knowing what I said was true. Shocker looked like she had eaten something foul. She nodded to Perry, who chuffed amusement before setting the files in front of my plate.

I wiped my hands. Took up the folder on top, opened it, not intending to read it just yet. "What Eddy said about the OGs was correct. They take care of business and make sure no unnecessary BS results from their enterprises. But I don't agree with what he said about the Two-Eleven and their allies." I closed the files.

"What do you mean?" Bobby said, pushing his plate away, wiping his mouth and hands.

"They aren't all water heads. Some of them are very smart."

"OGs? That's the Old Viet Mafia leaders, right?" Ace wanted to clarify.

"Right," I said. "I know one of the OGs. He can help us. But I can't go see him without an escort." I looked at my girl.

"Big Guns?" Blondie raised a perfect brow, tapping a napkin to her full lips.

I nodded, balling my fist to keep from slipping my hand under her shirt. "Text him, will you? We need to set up a meeting with Trung."

Shocker frowned. "That name sounds familiar."

"Trung is one of the more common Vietnamese names, though there's nothing common about this guy. He runs the Dragon Family."

"Sounds like a big deal," Shocker said.

I looked at her. "The Dragon Family is huge, with many subsets and thousands of members in most major cities. Their counterparts, the Tiger Society, are equally as powerful and ubiquitous. The Two-Eleven are a subset of the Tiger Society."

"That sounds like something you'd see on TV, not around here," Perry declared.

"Oh, they're very real. Those organizations are largely in legit business, but have numerous factions involved in every criminal activity you can think of, and then some. Think about all the cocaine, marijuana and ecstasy on the Coast. These guys have been the main suppliers and distributors for over a decade, yet you rarely hear of them getting busted. They're smart. They pay off the Narcotics Task Force to avoid raids, and can usually get their guys off the hook, if they do get popped. They take care of their own."

"So, they're organized with vast resources and manpower, and us five are going to spank them and clean up their mess?" Shocker said in a tone that was more playful than skeptical. Bobby and Ace looked at her and smiled.

"Us *six*," Perry corrected. Shocker grinned at him.

"I've got nothing better to do at the moment," I replied, trying not to show how excited I was. This promised to be a complicated bitch of danger, and I couldn't wait to get started. I rubbed my hands together. Blondie, an addict for peril herself, smiled and wriggled next to me. I stuck my hand on her leg, squeezed. She pinched it merrily.

Perry raised his glass of tea. "To Eddy's project. May that bastard's mission not get us all killed." Smiles and glasses raised around the table.

Shocker drank, looked at her guys. "I hope I don't regret this. I'm still not sure about following the President of the United Streets of America." She jerked a thumb at me.

I pushed my shoulders back, smoothed the front of my shirt, straightened an imaginary tie. In a tone dripping with ego I said, "President, bitch."

Perry insisted on cleaning the dishes, and we all thanked him for the exquisite meal before heading out the front door, the girls hugging him, guys gripping his hand. He held it for us. "Keep me informed. When you guys need first-aid or some extra muscle you know where to find me."

"Will do, Unc." I said shaking his hand. Turned to walk to my bike. Recalling something, I spun back around, face apologetic. "The hall bathroom?"

"What about it?" Perry scowled.

"Sanitize the sink."

"Damn kids," he muttered, closing the door.

The driveway looked like we were getting ready for a Cruisin' the Coast event. Shocker, Ace and Big Swoll rolled out of the garage in a *bad ass* '59 El Camino, red and gray with 20" custom wheels. The garage door cycled down, shutting. The sound of the engine made me want to run over and hump the hood. The big block monster under there, breathing at least 550hp, caressed every part of me that loves to go fast.

Blondie admired Shocker's ride with that jealous-envious glower I was unused to but was beginning to like. Reminded me of days before I knew her, when girls competed for my attention, doing everything short of cutting each other's throats. *Ah...lovely memories.*

Blondie's '52 Ford was a beautiful machine, the dark purple shining, fluent tones reflecting stars in the black sky. She climbed in, shut the door. Started and revved the 600hp Ford Racing engine, Flowmaster turbo mufflers roaring, alive and eagerly seeking her touch on the throttle.

My grin decided it was permanent. I waved at Blondie, made a motion for her to roll down the window. Handed Eddy's files in, then held my bag of coke open in front of her boobies. My pinkie darted out and stole a tickle. One long green nail thumped my hand, then disappeared into the baggie, to her nose, her sniffing of the bump delicate and precise. She blew me a kiss, flipped me off, and I loaded up two large bumps for myself before pocketing the drug, donning my helmet, mounting the Suzuki. "Here comes trouble!" I warned the public.

Shocker shouted at me. "Where's the garage?"

"Off ninety, in Pass Christian."

She waved, executed a three-point turn with ease, the El Camino's fat dual exhaust pipes hyperventilating a big cam lope as she shifted gears, sound deafening as she raced down the long driveway, onto the road next to the beach, Blondie hot on her tail.

Reveling in the fresh drip that raped my senses, I had to exercise great restraint in not leaving black marks on the cement, speeding after the two crazy women that will surely attract every law enforcement officer between here and Hancock County.

We caught a red light at the intersection of Highway 90 and Washington Avenue. The F100 and El Camino lined up side by side at the wide white strip. I stopped several car lengths behind them to avoid flying debris from their massive tires. The girls glanced at each other, profiles a collage of reds, yellows, from the play of lights, eyes indistinct though abstractly determined. They kept a close eye on the traffic, anticipating the green flash that would start their drag race.

What is it about red lights that makes us want to race the driver next to us? It was a thrilling pleasure to be sure, but one they shouldn't indulge at this point. Shocker and

Ace were major fugitives, and Blondie wasn't exactly loved by the local heat herself. I just shook my head, amazed by the energy women have when competing against each other. *And they have the nerve to scoff at men who do incredibly stupid things in the name of status.*

Mystifying.

Blondie had rebuilt the 429 in the Ford herself, and I'm willing to bet the Shocker had fabricated her entire El Camino. If I remember correctly, she used to own a mechanic shop in Woolmarket, Custom Ace, before she and her husband were imprisoned four years ago. These two crazy goddamn women had already contested their fighting skills. Now they'll contest their Who's the Better Builder and Driver skills.

My Johnson decided he didn't need sex to be in Heaven and swelled with divine euphoria as the dynamic angels left ridiculously long black marks across the intersection, green light blurring overhead as I walked a wheelie after them, giggling like a mad man.

The Fort Bayou Bridge was about a quarter mile ahead, the foot of it a perfect Finish line for their race. Evidently, the girls weren't satisfied with a tie, blasting over the bridge without a thought of slowing, weaving around several cars, blaring horns drowned out by the bellowing exhaust of the two big blocks, sound waves rocketing out over the dark water.

My tires hit the grate of the drawbridge, the rear Pirelli momentarily losing traction on the steel, the bike's engine racing, rubber gripping firmly again, popping up the front-end as I rolled on concrete once more. "PRESIDENT, BITCH!" I screamed in my helmet, shifting gears.

The wide lanes provided plenty of room to maneuver around the few vehicles that were out this early in the morning. Numerous businesses, medical plazas, gas stations blipped by, peripheral tracers reminiscent of a great acid trip. A quick glance at the speedo' told me that we were going 140 mph, the girls just ahead of me, neck-and-neck, their hot rods evenly matched. Both had slammed, NASCAR-like suspensions, wide tires and aerodynamics that loved high speeds, tricky corners, and plenty of courage behind the wheel.

A curve ahead gently sloped to the right, a major intersection with Lemoyne Boulevard perpendicular to it. As dangerous as that was, it didn't worry me. The Sheriff's substation we had to pass to get there did, though. Our 150 mph trio blazed by the station with enough noise to rival the sonic boom of a fighter jet, surely rousing the doughnut eaters that called themselves deputies. The intersection had a few cars, none in our way, red lights barely registering in my senses, a straightaway showing Interstate 10 mere seconds away. Speedway on the right, Denny's on the left, the girls' brake lights beaming as they slowed for the on-ramp.

As I leaned to follow I swiveled my head and saw flashing light bars on several Crown Victoria's racing in our direction, far behind us. "Aw. Whittle piggies can't keep up with the big hogs." Eyes front, I merged onto the interstate, jaw beginning to cramp from holding a tight grin.

It was 1:00 a.m., traffic thin but not completely out of the way. The big Hayabusa vibrated pleasantly in 6th gear, RPMs at 9,000 and climbing, nearing 160 mph, vision oscillating from the winds buffeting the bike's wide engine fairing. It was a chore to concentrate on what was ahead of me rather than what was right in front of me. Maintaining speed vision is intrinsic to racing of any sort. A racer in their prime has the cognitive ability to handle it much longer and accurately than a person past their ideal thinking years. An experienced young racer can really push the envelope, stay in front of the competition, on the edge, if they have the self-assurance and boldness, the *want*, to be superior to all others at all costs. Those who fear injury come in last.

I felt that bold emotion coursing through my veins now and knew the angels in front of me must feel it even stronger, them being in actual competition at present. The rush could be extremely exhausting; Indy car and NASCAR drivers lose up to eight pounds during a single race. However, considering the physical conditioning of Blondie and Shocker, I didn't think fatigue would be an issue... But the state trooper we just passed was a different matter, a potentially dangerous issue.

Letting off the throttle I slowed to 75 mph, which seemed like 10 mph after going a buck-sixty. Weaved into the right lane between a Peterbuilt and a sedan, allowing the trooper to catch up then pass me. Jumping back into the left lane I hit a toggle on my handgrip that switched off my lights, shadowing the headlamp and license plate so the cop wouldn't see me come up behind him or make a note of my plate as I raced past.

With my left hand I unsheathed my straight razor, flicked open the blade. Downshifted and sped up behind, then alongside the trooper's Crown Vic, left leg nearly touching his right passenger door. I grunted, swinging the blade down, slicing through the rear tire, immediately leaning right to avoid the car careening into me, his tire shredded, rubber flying in all directions, peppering the cars in the right lane, whose drivers looked at me in shocked disbelief. I sheathed my blade, waved to my audience and flicked the lights back on, getting back in the throttle, the cop's light minuscule and fading in my mirror as I tried to catch up to the girls.

My chest pressed proudly into the fuel tank. I sputtered a silly laugh. Why the hell did I ever quit doing this? I'm so good at it.

I snorted, swallowed, shook my head.

I wasn't able to catch up, nearly a mile behind after

neutralizing the cop. I exited into Pass Christian, zipped south to Highway 90, and was at the parking garage in minutes. It was six stories high, on a corner of a residential street that ended at the highway. A couple of oak trees bristling in the median out front, dark and barren around the sides. Empty lot out back separating it from a condo complex of recent build. Traffic was surprisingly thick in the four lanes between me and the beach, moon partly covered by black clouds over the Gulf.

I began to turn into the garage entrance, but braked quickly, feet touching asphalt, jerking my head around to see Blondie and Shocker talking to a kid that wore some kind of billboard over his head, the square of plywood hanging from his neck to the top of his shoes. They both wore pouty, Aw Poor Baby expressions, leaning over to listen to the boy whine about something.

"Fuck. What drama hell is this now?" I sighed, irritated that the electrifying race had ended and we were back to having feelings again.

I put the bike on its kickstand, killed the ignition and pocketed the keys. Took off my helmet, hooked it on the handlebars, inhaling the fresh sea air deeply. Walked towards the women. I rounded the corner and stopped short. Bobby's mountainous frame stood next to Ace's lamppost physique, their backs against the gray concrete of the first-story wall, watching the scene with amusement. I gestured, *What's the business?*

Bobby smiled. "That kid's dad made him stand by the highway wearing that sign. The ladies took offense."

I couldn't see the sign from here. "What's it say?"

Ace frowned, said, "I lie, steal, and sell drugs."

"Really?" I grinned, stuck my hands in my pockets. "My kind of kid."

Bobby shook his head at me in disappointment. "That kid's gonna end up in prison." He frowned at the thought.

"The father must be a real jive turkey. You don't publicly shame your kids like this. It's the parents' fault that boy is lying and breaking laws in the first place."

"Makes sense," I agreed, unable to offer any insight. I've never been parented or done any parenting.

I looked back at the kid. He pointed to the back of the garage, head down in guilt, and both girls looked in that direction with furious mugs. They eased the billboard from around his neck, dropped it. Shocker took his hand and they marched quickly around the building with purpose.

"Uh-oh," Ace said smiling. "I know that look."

"Yeah." I matched his cheer. "Someone's going to get an attitude adjustment."

"Come on," Bobby said, teeth bright white in the shadows. "The father must be out back. We'll block him if he tries to escape."

We followed the giant around the other side of the garage, peeked around the corner and saw a car parked in the empty lot, a tan Nissan Sentra, a man of middle-age in the driver's seat. He spotted the women and his son stalking toward him, got out, standing with hands on waist like he was going to assert some kind of authority over the situation. I had to clamp a hand over my mouth to hold back a shout of laughter.

"Are you Greg, this boy's father?" Shocker demanded, the three of them stopping right in front of the man, who closed the door, interior light clicking off.

"Yes. What are you doing with Carl?" he replied in an argumentative tone. He was about six-two, two-sixty, a lifetime pizza and beer guy with thick black hair curled over his ears, shiny from the street lights illuminating the lot.

Blondie's fury was a sight to behold. She took a step closer to Greg and snarled, "The question is, what are *you* doing with Carl? You piece of shit. Do you have any idea how much damage you are doing to your son? He's going to be fucked up on psych meds for the rest of his life because of *your* ignorant ass!"

I'm pretty sure her *Psychology Today* magazines didn't say that exactly, but her version was much more effective at getting the point across, don't you agree?

Greg puffed out his chest. "Now, that's none of your business, whoever you-"

Crack!

Blondie's slap was nearly too fast to see. Greg's large head bucked to the side, he staggered, and Shocker darted in with a straight-right to his pepperoni-and-extra-cheese gut, grunting as it thudded deep into him. She reset, he cried out, voice cut off as his breathing failed, doubling over, arm shooting out to grab the car for support. Knees crunching painfully in the gravel. The kid's eyes popped wide. I laughed, Ace and Bobby doing the same. The girls and Carl looked up at us. We walked over to join the party.

Greg, trying to stay balanced while kneeling, coughed painfully, face a gold-scarlet in the light. Both girls stood over him with tight fists, obviously wanting to do him something worse. Because they were too emotionally involved I decided to add a clear head to the situation. The guy had been disciplined, though hadn't learned his lesson. He needed to know worse would happen if he did something like this again. And besides, this was a great opportunity to score some points with my girl, get her to see that I do have a heart when it comes to kids.

I stepped over to Greg, put a foot on his back and shoved him face down to the ground. He cursed out a breath. I leaned over and jerked his wallet from his back pocket. Opened it. Removed the driver's license. Slipped the BlackBerry from my pants. Snapped a pic of his ID, reinserted it in the wallet, tossed it down. I gestured at Bobby and he happily snatched Greg up like he weighed nothing. I got right in the asshole's face.

"Listen up, pal. You're fortunate these ladies don't go full *Colombiana* on your ass. If your kid would benefit from seeing you get beaten to death," I grinned wolfishly, "it just wouldn't be your day. You can thank the Odds there isn't any pro-patricide literature out there."

Blondie sighed behind me and I thought, *Okay, maybe I could have phrased that differently.*

"However, I'm not so forgiving. If I have to give you a tune-up you'll get far more than a slap and a gut punch." I feinted a jab at his face. He flinched, started shaking. "I have your ID info, and plan to keep tabs on you and Carl." Turning to the boy I said, "How old are you?"

"Twelve," he murmured with his head down.

"Look at me." He looked up, brown eyes wide under a shag of dirty blonde hair. Nose and chin strong, freckles on his cheeks, and a black eye, the real reason the girls were so incensed. I planned to lecture him on selling dope later, and the ABCs of Thievery. But had something else in mind for now. "You want a job?"

He looked at his dad. Back to me. "I guess so."

"See this garage?" He nodded. "I own it. I need someone to clean it twice a week. You'll be sweeping eight hours a day on Mondays and Fridays for two hundred dollars."

"And when you start school again, we'll work out a different schedule, honey," Blondie told him, stroking his hair.

I smiled at her, *He goes to school???* Carl took a breath, licked his lips. I told him, "Come see me here on the top floor, next Monday at seven o'clock. Okay?" He nodded yes, eyes wide again. I turned back to Greg. "That's okay with you, Dad."

"I, uh-"

"Shut up." I slapped him. "I wasn't asking you." I stood there uncertainly for a moment, thinking fast. I glanced at Blondie, who gave me her And??? look, like I was leaving something out. All I could think of was something I saw on TV about kids staying up too late. It was past this dude's bedtime, right? I said, "Why is Carl not in bed? It's nearly two a.m."

"It's complicated," Greg mumbled, grimacing, massaging his cheek.

"No, trying to pee with morning wood is complicated. Making sure your kid has a good night's sleep is simple." Another glance at Blondie earned me a *good enough* nod of approval. *I'll count that as she owes me one*, I thought, focusing on the jackass again. I nodded to Bobby. He released Greg, folded his arms.

I looked at the car, about to walk away, spotting a can of spray paint in the back seat. Glossy black that had been used to make the shame sign. I smiled wickedly. Opened the door, grabbed it.

As we walked back to the garage entrance, horns sounded repeatedly from motorists passing by the man standing in the median with a billboard hanging from his neck. I SHAME MY KID IN PUBLIC – HONK IF I AM A BITCH was painted in fresh shiny black on the new shame sign. Greg stood there, hair blowing around his embarrassed, humbled face. Carl, sitting on a branch high in an oak tree, looked down on his father with a satisfied smirk.

"Well, I'd say our first job as a team was a success," Ace said smugly. His lanky walk reminded me of a praying mantis.

I straddled the Suzuki. "That's the fourth most interesting thing to arouse me tonight."

"Fourth?" Blondie queried. Everyone stopped to listen. Shocker glanced at my crotch too, presumably, see how literal I was being.

"Yes." I ticked off on my fingers. "First, a meth shooter attempted to rob me before I met you at Eddy's." I looked at Shocker. "I checked him," I told her, snapping a check-hook, the same move she had used to disarm Blondie. I turned back to my girl. "Then I had the pleasure of fighting the girl-beast."

"Hey!" Shocker fumed. *"Girl-beast?!"*

I gave her my #1 Mr. Good Guy smile, held up a third digit, which just happened to be my middle finger. Her lips puckered, eyes narrowed. "Third, I had to slash a cop's tire, because you two nut cases just *had* to see who sported the better set of boobies behind the wheel."

She and Blondie looked at each other, at the sky, ground, Shocker slightly embarrassed, Blondie smiling. *Guess my girl won that round.* Blondie: 1. Shocker: 1.

Four fingers. "Then I got to slap a deadbeat dad and offer a job to a juvenile hustler." I inhaled deeply. Sighed. "Thank you for a highly stimulating evening, ladies and gents."

"It's not over yet, Babe." Blondie showed me her phone: A text from Big Guns. "He'll be here in five."

"Marvelous."

Everyone got into their respective vehicles. We drove up the ramps, fluorescent lights bright on every floor, the chrome of our machines glinting off the cars filling the first three levels, exhaust deafening in the confined space. The next two levels were sparse of cars, the sections reserved for long-term parking. Stopping at the bottom of the top-level ramp, I hit a button on my phone. There was a heavy *clunk* from deep inside the concrete walls, forged steel bolts retracting. The vault-type door in front of us cycled open on a massive track from left to right. Another clunk when it stopped, open. Moonlight and stars greeted us as we drove up and out on the roof.

The top floor wasn't for parking; it was our playground. We kept several toys up here and maintained three work stations that we used to construct everything from welding jigs to sophisticated robotics. Two steel sheds, each twenty-five square feet, stood on either side of a canopied picnic area, floodlights lighting up two long tables with benches and a gas grill, all gleaming stainless steel. Behind that was a fifteen foot cinder block tower, a small observatory with a high-powered telescope and infrared and ultraviolet equipment. We called it our "Trippin' Tower."

Ever see shooting stars on acid? Put "LSD and telescope" on your Things To Do Before I Die list.

In front of one shed was a runway with orange guide lights anchored to the concrete. For my drone. The other shed held tools of various specs, a veritable lab that any craftsman would salivate over. That was Station #1. The tables under the canopy were Stations #2 and #3. Nearly every project would have components, tools and cables strewn out over every station, in an assembly line. Everything was clean and put away for now, though.

We parked by the sheds. Got out, doors closing, their normal *thunk* swallowed by the freedom of open air, a breezy black night. Shocker and her guys looked around in astonishment. She said, "Holy Shit. What do you guys do up here?"

"Get high, mostly," I answered. She frowned. Blondie tittered, walking towards the tables. I added, "We also engineer whatever contraptions that happen to be schemed up by our drug-enhanced minds."

"Uh-huh. I guessed as much. Eddy mentioned that you were taught by Pete Eagleclaw. I've always admired his motorcycle designs."

"You built cars, right?"

"Mmm-hmm. Had my own shop for a while. I honestly don't miss it. Miss doing tattoos, though." She sighed.

I looked at her right shoulder. A Champion-brand spark plug was tattooed there, colors and shading realistic, rays of blue and white spitting out of the plug's electrode. No other skin art could possibly fit her better. "I've seen work from your parlor, Tattoology. World-class."

"Boss, right?" She smiled, and I returned it. Another sigh. "That's all in the past. It's been all about the kids and making sure we leave no trails for the feds ever since our escape."

"No trails, hmm," I said thinking about the train of cops that was just chasing her. "Where do you live now?"

She didn't answer, looking around. Pointed to four one-foot square steel plates that were recessed in the concrete. "Is that a car lift?"

I nodded, letting her divert me. "Hydraulic cylinders."

"Nice," Bobby said smiling. "You could do a lot up here."

"That fractal antenna looks handy," Ace observed, pointing to a small apparatus jutting from the top of the observatory, a steel wire, multipurpose transmitter-receiver that looked like a large spider web. "You could intercept any frequency with that thing. Satellites, cell phones, law enforcement channels. Cool." He grinned in a manner that indicated he had a little criminal in him. It was then I decided to like the geeky bastard.

"'Handy is what we were shooting for," I told him. Cool wind blew hair in my eyes. I smoothed it over my head. Whipped out my BlackBerry and hit the garage app, typed in a quick command. One of the sheds to our right buzzed, the rolling door began cycling open, interior lights illuminating a small airplane. I walked over to it, licking my lips. You know that feeling you have when you get to show off something really cool to your pals? Imagine having built that "something" yourself, and, as far as it being cool, it was fucking liquid nitrogen.

"That's a *drone*," Ace exclaimed, eyes bright in fascination.

Shocker's eyebrows couldn't possibly go any higher.

"Does it fly?"

I acted offended. "Do balls smell funny? Of course it flies."

Blondie patted my arm. I turned and she showed me some pills in her palm. Two 10 mg Valium. She popped them in my mouth. *All she needs is a nurse outfit...* She gave me a drink from her water bottle and said, "Chill pill, Babe. You'll need to calm yourself if you plan on flying her. You remember what happened last-"

I kissed her to cut her off.

She laughed. Stroked my cheek. "I'll go meet Big G while you handle it up here."

Her perfect rump attracted my hand like a powerful magnet sticking to high-quality alloy. The affectionate smack caused her to yelp. She spun on her toe, throwing a hook that I ducked. She harrumphed, glowered and shook her fist, then stalked over to the ramp entrance to meet our associate.

"So what happened last time?" Bobby asked me, arms folded over his pink bodybuilder tank, smiling hugely.

I grumbled, "An old woman shot it down with a twelve-gauge. I was shooting video of her husband's marijuana field."

"Ha!"

The distinct *brrraattt* of a Honda V-Tec engine could be heard racing up the garage ramp, tires chirping faintly. A moment later Big Guns' lime green Prelude eased through the entry like an alien spacecraft cautiously scouting the earthly terrain. The wide body kit, barely clearing the ground, looked like it might start blinking and looking around with some sort of laser eyes. Black superturismo wheels and low-profile tires completely filled the wheel wells. He parked next to Blondie's Ford, enormous chrome exhaust pipe buzzing, going quiet as he killed the ignition and stepped out. Blondie hugged him. They turned in my direction.

Big Guns wasn't tall for a Vietnamese. But he was certainly one of the most muscular Asians I've ever seen. At five-five, one-ninety, he looked much heavier than he actually was. Jet black hair shaved on the sides, short and spiky up top. Hooded eyes over a wide nose, thick lips. Brown-gold skin sporting a colorful dragon that wrapped around his entire right arm, guns and girls tatted on his left, vintage Asian gangster. Loose Silver Tab jeans sagging slightly with a wide black belt. Lugz boots. Plain gray tank top that showed off his flat stomach and stout, vascular muscles. His serious face split into a wide smile when he saw me, silver teeth blinging chrome in the moon light. "Razor! You cracker bastard."

"Good to see you, little yellow man." We gripped hands, embraced. Stepped back. "Are you getting shorter?"

"Nah. You are getting skinnier." He flexed one of his guns, biceps jumping up like a veined baseball. Crossed his arms, nodded at our other guests. "You got me surrounded. Who are the squares?"

I gave Shocker a meaningful look. It was up to her how she wanted to introduce her crew. She quirked a brow in question. I nodded an affirmative. Big Guns could be trusted; being a sometimes fugitive himself, he knew the meaning of discretion, and certainly wouldn't do anything stupid like turn them in for reward money.

Shocker looked to be grinding her teeth in hesitation. Finally she said, "I'm Shocker. This is Ace and Bobby." Her guys jerked their heads up in greeting.

Big Guns had no idea who they were. His mouth flashed silver at them. "Big G. You must be significant if Razor and Goldilocks let you into their lair."

Shocker frowned in response. Her guys chewed over the statement.

Were they significant? My subconscious asked.

Odd how I didn't even hesitate to bring them up here.

Enough preamble. "Let's get down to business," I said, motioning for everyone to follow me into the drone shed.

The plane had a matte black exterior, aluminum and carbon fiber fuselage. The wing span was an even sixteen feet. It looked like a miniature Mitsubishi Zero, the Japanese fighters from World War II. The high-powered camera attached to the underbelly indicated its primary purpose: spying. Behind the propeller, on each side, were engine covers that housed a 125 hp rotary. A Wankel engine. Airbrushed on either one were demons with dragonfly wings, dark gray, ghostly over the black base. The evil entities looked to be writhing excitedly through the air, in ecstasy, teeth gnashing and claws ripping into the shady mission they flew towards.

Shocker admired the artwork, said, "What's her name?"

"Demonfly," I responded, walking around my current favorite creation to a large steel desk. Sat in the chair behind it. Blondie ushered them to the couch adjacent to the desk, walked over and plopped in my lap, chair squeaking a protest. Bobby, Ace and Big Guns took places on the couch, burgundy leather, no pillows.

Narrowing her eyes at me, Blondie, then the couch, Shocker said, "I think I'll stand."

Yes. We have done mucho freaky-deaky on that couch, my smile and shrug said to her. I looked at my Viet friend. "We need a meet with Trung."

His hooded eyes went to mere slits as he pondered my request. In a firm, decisive voice he said, "I can get you in. Maybe Blondie. No one else. Security is tight these days." His eyes tightened. "And you will call him *Anh Long.*"

The "no one else" in the shed looked unhappy about that. I said to Shocker, "I'll go talk to *Anh Long* and see what the Dragon Family's position is on our objective."

"*Anh Long?*"

Big Guns turned to her. "That's a formal title for the head of the Dragon Family. *Anh* means Elder Brother. *Long* is dragon. Trung is the head of the DF."

"Ah."

"Thank you," I told the Viet expert. He bowed with mock solemnity, making the girls laugh. I looked around at everyone, turning serious. "We'll need *Anh Long*'s support if we hope to succeed in this. If we start an operation on their turf without permission, we'll have their enmity as well as the Tiger Society's."

"Not good," Bobby remarked.

"Right. The OGs don't normally work with outsiders, especially on business between Families. But considering what's at stake, and all the people that could be affected if the enemy takes over, I think *Anh Long* will be open-minded."

"Let's hope so. I'd hate to bump heads with him, too," Shocker said in a deadly quiet voice. Her expression told everyone she planned on taking out the trash regardless of who helped or got in her way. Ace and Bobby looked from her to us, matching her determination. Big Guns eyed her warily, her ripped physique and boldness breaking through his deadpan demeanor.

A woman after my own heart, I grinned at her. "I believe you and I will be pals." She looked skeptical. Blondie tensed in my lap. I tried to stroke her leg, and just avoided getting a plug of skin pinched out of my hand.

"You guys are going to need tech support," Ace chimed in, fingers typing in the air. "I can handle that."

Blondie looked at him curiously. "You have a rig?" she said, meaning a computer setup capable of more than just updating Facebook or downloading porn.

He gave a secret smile. "Oh yeah. I have a Wrecker."

I wasn't sure what that meant, but it pleased my girl. She twisted around. Said to me, "I believe he and I will be pals."

I reached up and gave one of her nipples a quick twist between my fingers, too fast for anyone to notice. Enjoying her sudden inhalation, I addressed our team. "It's late. How about we meet back here at noon? Ace and Blondie can collaborate on the tech side of the job while the rest of us devise a war strategy."

"Sounds good," Shocker yawned. Everyone agreed, standing.

As the roaring exhaust of the El Camino and Prelude faded down the garage levels, I picked my girl up, carried her over to the couch, threw her down on it and jerked my shirt off. Unbuckled my belt. "No sleep for the wicked," I growled low.

She chortled agreement, unzipping me.

My Johnson twirled around in happy expectation.

V. Our New Recruit

"Oh, I'm so wet! Give it to me now, motherfucker!" Blondie cried out, lithe wicked arms reaching for me with eagerness. Mouth open in teased anger.

I tisked her. "Babe, if you keep up that attitude, I'm not going to give you the umbrella."

Rain poured forth from a gray summer sky, dimming the concrete of the parking garage and sidewalks, graying the sand of the beach we walked towards. We had finished our morning run, but canceled our usual workout on the heavy bag and punch mitts to get ready for our team meeting. Blondie had primped her hair, makeup, and dressed in a black halter top and camouflage skirt. The outfit showcased one delicious midriff, her long fit legs, sexy tapered calves, rock hard above black boots, sharp pointed toes with four-inch heels knocking wetly on the highway as we hurried across. I handed her the umbrella, saving her thirty minute hair and face job, allowing her to run ahead so I could admire the view.

The Gulf's water was excited, frothy waves pounding the sand, dark sky promising worse to come. Lightning made a spectacular show far out to the east over Cat Island. I ignored it. Blondie's heels held my attention. *There's just something about the sound of heels* ... No matter who wears them, Big Baby on Sexy Lady, when you hear them clacking down a hall or sidewalk you just have to look, knowing you'll see a set of jacked up legs and pumped up butt. "She's got legs. And she knows how to use them," I sang, jamming my trusty air guitar.

I was soaked as soon as she ran off. But I didn't mind. The white tank and Diesel jeans I wore weren't anything special. I'll just change again, as soon as we find the sack of weed she lost during our run.

"Found it!" she turned and yelled at me, walking in the sand awkwardly. Squatted down, plucked a Ziploc from the beach. "It fell out of my damn bra." She smiled, held up the treasure. The four inch baggie held half a dozen joints, rolling papers bright white inside the glistening plastic. The last of our stash. Losing it had terrified us.

I wiped my brow in relief. "Good find, Lean Meats. Now, get your blonde furred self over here. We have to make up for lost high time." I grinned in anticipation, pulled a chrome Zippo from my jeans.

We stood on the beach, twisting the umbrella around to block the wind and rain, smoking a joint the size of my thumb. *Wake and bake, bitch*, I exulted, gliding on the superb quality herb.

Cars passed on the highway, headlights obscured by the storm. One turned off on the road next to the garage, the blue-white Xenon lights directed at the entrance. I squinted, trying to see the vehicle more clearly. It was a dark green Scion FR-S, a cool little sports car with a boxer engine and 6-speed. Blondie nudged me, as curious as I was to see it up close, and we put out the doobie to amble across the flooded four-lane gauntlet, her negotiating the umbrella, holding my hand, trusting me to guide us through traffic.

We walked into the entrance, senses reasserting awareness now that we were out of the deluge. Blondie closed the umbrella. Shook her hair out over her shoulders. We looked around for the Scion, knowing it had to be on the first level; we watched for the headlights to appear on the second level, but they didn't.

The first level was nearly full, with only a few available slots. We followed the wet tire tracks, which abruptly ended in front of an empty slot, curving and crossing over one another, indicating the Scion had backed into the slot. *But it's empty.*

"What the fuck..." Blondie muttered, squinting hard.

I kept looking at the empty slots, the tracks, over and over, tripping, thinking that joint must've had more than THC in it, when Shocker appeared out of thin air in the slot with the tracks, not forty feet in front of us.

"Hi, guys," she said with a wave and brilliant grin. She closed the invisible door, and the air to her left *shimmered*, like a computer screen resolving an image, and dark green digital paint formed front-end, hood, fenders, then the rest of the car as if it were a hologram in 3D. Straight out of *Popular Science*. Tall concrete pillars blocked the lights, putting the slot in shadow, supplementing the effect.

We were stupefied. "Nice," I breathed. "Scion would pay a mint to have that in their commercials."

"Liquid crystal display. On a car," my girl said, impressed beyond belief.

The thin video screen covering the windshield rolled up into a slit in the roof. Ace stepped out of the driver's side, closed it. Walked over next to his girl, wide grin on his angular face. His blonde spikes seemed sharper. "I took a picture of your faces," the geek said, smug and pleased.

We walked over to the car, ignoring them for a moment, peering closely at the masterpiece in front of us. Ace was a hell of a materials scientist. The electroactive polymers he created for Shocker's compression sleeve were impressive, but this was downright mind-blowing.

Blondie said, "You have cameras on the back of the car?"

Ace nodded. "Integrated in the taillights and tag lights, the undercarriage, and in the door handles. The paint is not real paint, of course. I can select dozens of colors or graphic art designs from the program menu. Its pixels, in molded LCD monitors. The body panels are made from a clear, very durable plastic and carbon nanotube material, highly polished to look like clear coat. The LCDs are behind the panels, perfectly contoured to form the lines of the car. The exterior is essentially a giant TV screen." He gestured at the rear of the car. "The cameras capture whatever is behind, under and beside the car. A modified processor with a simple algorithm governs the image. The cameras also track movement, and the projections on the front, sides, and roof will adjust relative to the direction of the person or other vehicle the program is trying to hide from. The rear of the car is completely visible, so I have to make sure the front of the car faces whoever I'm avoiding. Shadows help, as you can see. The car is visible in bright light."

"I fucking love it," I declared. Blondie murmured consent.

He shrugged, hands deep in his gray cargo pants. "The technology has been around for years. Just not on cars. It's probably illegal."

Shocker inhaled proudly, cut her eyes lovingly at her man. She told us, "He can't drive fast, so there's no way he'll ever outrun the cops. We had to come up with something else, a way he could hide from them if he gets chased."

"I'd say you hit the bull's-eye," I replied. I ran my fingers over the fender. The "paint" looked like it had a very thick clear coat, which made it very glossy, but you'd never guess it was a digital screen under a meta-material. "I love anti-authority devices," I said with emotion.

"What other materials have you developed?" Blondie quizzed the geek, stepping closer to him. His skinny chest inflated his blue Apple Computers shirt, face and arms becoming animated as they began conversing in Nano tech.

I motioned for Shocker to walk with me. Our squad headed up the ramps, rain muffled then loud as we opened the door to the sixth level. We hurried to the canopied area between the sheds, through it to the drone hanger, collective sighs huffing once we were out of the rain again.

I left the door open, the sound and smell refreshing, breeze cool. Blondie and Ace sat on the couch, still chattering away. I gave Shocker the chair behind the desk and stood. "Where's Bobby?" I said.

"He has a wife and kids, plus a paint and body business to run," Shocker answered. Her brown hair was in a tight ponytail, hazel eyes bright over a piggish-but-cute nose. She wore a black warm-up suit with "Adidas" embroidered in pink stitching on the sleeves and legs. She folded her arms, leaned back. "He'll be there when we need him."

I nodded thoughtfully. "Big Guns will meet us at *Anh Long's* place shortly. Have you thought about how you want to do this job?"

She frowned, held up a fist. "I only know one way to take care of business with gangsters. Fire with fire. Stupid with stupider."

My canines lengthened. I gave a smile fit for the cover of *Savage*. "Team." I held my fist out, she bumped it.

She thinks just like you, my subconscious observed, surprised but not displeased.

A familial feeling struck me. In another life this chick could have been my sister. *Or more appropriately, you could have been her brother*, my subconscious corrected, reminding me of her status.

I tried not to scowl at that, said, "We need to set an example for the Two-Eleven and OBG, and make sure they know why they are being attacked and what they can do to make it stop."

"OBG?" Ace said.

"Oriental Baby Gangsters. When they turn eighteen they call themselves Oriental Boy Gangsters. We have to make them-"

"Stop being such greedy little pricks," Blondie said, face tightening.

"And fucking up our hometowns," Ace added, glancing

at Shocker, Blondie.

Everyone chuckled. "You don't have to be vulgar to be a part of the team," I told him. He had no business trying to curse. He sounded like a lame, though I decided to keep that to myself in the interest of team morale.

Blondie had a hand to her mouth. Shocker smiled at Ace, at us. She elaborated, "He picked up some bad habits in prison." She put a hand on her chest and exaggerated, "I swear he doesn't get that from me."

Ace looked defensive. "I can curse better than that," he muttered. We burst out laughing. Blondie grabbed my shoulder and slapped her thigh. My abs cramped. "Well, I *can!*" he yelled.

More laughter.

"Burnt circuits," he grumbled, sulky.

~ ~ ~

"I hurt myself today / to see if I still feel / I focus on the pain / the only thing that's real," Seven Dust with Johnny Cash jammed from the Scion's stereo system. Blondie and I sat in the backseat, her warm leg touching mine in the small space. I kept looking at the camo' pattern of her skirt. It was a real chore to keep from finding out the pattern of her panties underneath. She wouldn't tell, the vixen, preferring that I find some devious means of doing so, while she countered my attempts with sass or blistering jabs. It was fun and games to her. I, on the other hand, took this very seriously.

I just had to *know*.

Dammit!

Ace turned a curve sharply, giving me reason to lean. I flopped over in Blondie's lap, hand reaching, and was head-butted in the ear.

"Ow! Fine." I sat up and rubbed my head.

She smiled, flicked imaginary dust off her skirt. Pursed her lips primly.

The rain had relented to a light drizzle, sky beginning to lighten. The FR-S handled the slick roads with perfect repose, sound-insulated interior smelling strongly of new car, MP3 playing a range of rock music we all enjoyed. We turned into a large neighborhood of small houses, import cars in every driveway, half of them customized, indicative of a primarily young Asian community. Turned right, right again, and spotted Big Guns' Prelude parked in the street with eight other cars in front of a brick house that looked to be hosting a party.

The front door was open, two almond-eyed hotties clustered next to it, giggling, three young men enticing them loudly in Vietnamese from a wooden porch swing to the right, crepe myrtle trees green and pink in front of them. The guys saw us, stood abruptly and motioned for the girls to go inside. They did without question, closed the door quickly.

As Ace and Shocker got out and held the seats up for us to shimmy out, Blondie stepped on something plastic, heel cracking the unseen item on the tiny dark floorboard. "Shit! I'm sorry," she said, stepping out of the car, leaning back in to inspect the damage.

Ace tried to jump in front of her. "Don't worry about it," he said too late.

Blondie stood, holding a box set of DVDs, smiling beautifully. She read the titles out loud. "*The Art of Sex Positions. The Art of Oral Sex.* And *The Art of Orgasms.*" She turned to her pal, swatted his shoulder and squealed, "You dirty dog!" She put them back in the car.

Ace's face had turned a darker shade after every title. He looked over the roof at his girl. "I, uh ... We ... You," he stuttered.

I laughed at Shocker's expression. She had no knowledge of the DVDs. I jerked my head up at the geek. "I can tell you some things they don't put on DVD. *Fifty*

Shades of Razor." Now it was Blondie's turn to blush. I indicated the three armed Viet soldiers walking toward us. "Game faces now, sex faces later. What do you say?"

They nodded quickly. Shut the doors.

The men wore baggy jeans and dress shirts. Long gold and silver necklaces, boots, and skateboard shoes. One had bright red bangs framing his chiseled face. All wore Who The Fuck Are You? scowls.

I matched their demeanor, stepped in front of my team and demanded, "Where is Big Guns?"

"Who wants to know?" Red Bangs said, English heavily accented.

I looked each of them in the eye. "Razor."

Their manner changed instantly. Eyes widening, mouths loosening, hands finding hair or clothes to straighten. Blondie *hmmpted* in satisfaction. Red Bangs turned to his left, commanding the youngest of the trio, *"Kiem thang xuon bu,"* find Big Guns.

He hurried off, boots squishing across the wet lawn. Red Bangs and his partner had no small talk, opting to inspect Ace's car while stealing glances at the girls. Young Vietnamese were serious about import cars, and the FR-S was a threat to their Hondas and Acuras in style and performance. Scion, a subsidiary of Toyota, was only partly accepted by these guys. Tolerated. They looked at the machine with a mixture of skepticism and admiration.

They'd really get their auto-panties riled if they saw it disappear, I mused.

My crew remained quiet as well, listening to the party sounds coming from the backyard. There was some kind of contest in play, maybe a gambling tournament, shouts, jeers, and laughter voiced eloquently in their foreign tongue. Curiosity began to eat me, and I couldn't wait for my muscle-bound friend to get his ass out here so we could go join the action.

Big Guns and the messenger appeared through the front door. My friend smiled silver at us, turned and barked an order to the messenger, who hurried off to another task. The Viet gangster motioned for us to come inside, scowling at Red Bangs and his partner. Both dropped their eyes in their superior's presence, hurriedly searched us four guests for weapons, patting our armpits, waists, ankles. Then they sat on the porch swing once more, back on guard duty.

Ace closed the door behind us softly. Pop music played from a TV, living room yellow with white trim, tastefully furnished with Ikea's best. We followed Big Guns into the dining room. He turned and pointed at Shocker, Ace, at the living room. "You two have to stay here," he said apologetically.

They made disgruntled expressions, but complied, sitting next to each other on a blue sofa, rejects at a VIP event.

Through the sliding glass door in the kitchen was a patio with white plastic furniture, an umbrella table with six older Vietnamese men, two with young women in their laps, stacks of cash and writing tablets in front of them. They were cheering, laughing, heads twisted to the left, gesturing wildly as their girls chortled and squirmed in tight shorts. They quieted when we walked out, shut the glass door. Hooded eyes stared us down. We ignored them, looking at the source of the ruckus: a three foot tall circular ring of plywood, twelve feet in diameter, surrounded by whooping and hollering Asians of all ages, mostly male, a couple grandmas. Eyes on the cockfight in progress, they didn't notice our approach.

A wooden fence encompassed the quarter-acre yard, tall thick bushes lining it for additional privacy. A small stone statue of Buddha, pot-bellied and grinning at the heavens, cast his charms from the center of a bird bath in the middle of the lawn, several small children playing under it with toy cars. Big Guns motioned for us to stand by the fence until the fight was over.

We didn't have to wait long. The dinosaur descendant's bokked loudly, furiously, one of them warbling in pain, the other in triumph, and half the men around the ring groaned at their loss. "*Cac* !" several spat, a word with a very amusing sound that translated to "shit" or "fuck." One winner, a thirty-something in khakis and heavy gold chains waved a wad of cash in his friend's faces. "*Du ma! Du ma!,*" he told them. "Fuck your mom," or "Shit, that's what's up," depending on the context. I laughed, feeling their energy. I love high stakes risk, and knew what it felt like to beat the Odds, and get scuffed by them.

A man older than everyone else at the ring noticed us and stared for a moment, eyes slitted. He smiled suddenly. Fended off two women who clamored next to him, one holding his winnings, and walked over to us. Trung was around seventy, though it was hard to tell. He had one of those expressionless Asian faces that never accumulated wrinkles. The only sign of his age was from the sun he slaved under on shrimp boats before climbing to the top of the Dragon Family. He wore a plaid short-sleeve button-up, navy slacks and dark leather sandals. Hair gray, combed to the side. His smile was yellowed from decades of coffee, but friendly and powerful. The man didn't look fancy, but still managed to convey CHIEF somehow. I've had the pleasure of his acquaintance twice before, and was equally impressed those times as well.

He stopped several feet from us. Nodded to his subordinate. "*Em Hung,*" young protégé, he greeted Big Guns formally, voice warm but commanding. He looked at me, Blondie, eyes nearly black. He spoke perfect English, like a news journalist. "Razor, what brings you and this lovely golden warrior to my family's home?"

Blondie smiled at his charm. I inclined my head

respectfully and said, "To make a request, *Anh Long*." He waved a hand for me to go on. "We are going to put the brakes on the Two-Eleven and their allies. They are on a destructive path that has been unfortunate for many people, as I'm sure you know. We want to stop them before they reach a point where they can't be stopped."

Anh Long was quiet for several seconds, assessing the three of us. He said to his protégé, "Who is 'we'?"

Big Guns bobbed his head. "Razor, Blondie. A fighter that calls herself Shocker. Her boyfriend Ace, who is a tech specialist. And a bodybuilder named Bobby." He gave a small bow, smiled. "And myself, *Anh Long*."

"Hmm," he considered. "I would meet this Shocker." He folded his arms, seeming to know she was here and would discuss no more until she was present.

Big Guns hurried over to the patio, ducked through the sliding door and returned with the girl-beast in tow. In the unflattering warm up suit Shocker's appearance was deceptive. She looked athletic, sure, but no one would ever guess she was the baddest chick to ever put on gloves. She wore an uncertain, innocent look that belied her confident, violent nature. An act I admired so much that I tried the expression myself. It felt gay after a moment, so I quit.

Big Guns started to introduce her. The Elder Dragon said, "I know who Shocker is." He turned to her. She sucked in a breath. Big Guns looked confused while Blondie and I smiled. The old man chuckled. "Don't look so surprised, Miss Ares. After all, you were a celebrity to fight fans, which includes the decrepit Elder in front of you."

He looked very concerned about her panicked countenance. She looked ready to sprint for her life. He stepped closer and took her hand. "You have nothing to fear. No one here will bring you harm. I can assure you."

Shocker smiled, *Thanks*. Took a breath. "Pleasure to meet you, *Anh Long*."

81

"Oh, the pleasure is all mine. This is a treat. You make me feel like a young man asking for an autograph." She turned scarlet. He chuckled again, released her hand and looked around at us. "Now. What is it you require of the Dragon Family?"

"Permission, and someone good with a rifle," I said, eyeing him and Shocker. I had heard *Anh Long* was a kickboxing enthusiast, and good at it. I'm not surprised he follows boxing too, though I am surprised he seemed to know Shocker before even seeing her. *The messenger told him she was here,* I thought. Blondie and I are known boxers. Big Guns called her a "fighter." A lot can be inferred from that.

How many chicks called themselves Shocker?

"Permission to war against Tiger Society?" *Anh Long* said, clasping hands behind his back.

"That's right. Some of our fighting may happen on the DF's turf. We don't want any misunderstanding with your guys."

"I see." Instead of answering, he glanced at his watch, turned and waved a specific gesture at a kid who looked like a street urchin, skinny with dingy shorts, ragged sandals and a shirt with holes in it. The boy had been watching the Elder Dragon like a squire watches a king, eagerly awaiting his commands, hoping to anticipate them. He took a huge rooster out of a cage, held it out in front of him to avoid being clawed by the sharp steel spurs attached to its feet. Walked quickly over to kneel in front of his liege.

Anh Long knelt and stroked the rooster's head. The cone, the red Mohawk of skin that crowned a rooster's head, had been removed. It was a common practice, kept them from becoming snagged by spurs or pecked during battle. Same reason you don't see fighters with long hair; it's highly inconvenient when your opponent grabs a handful and steers you wherever they want. The feathers were white and black, golden brown, a few fringed with a gnarly purple that looked airbrushed. It was a magnificent animal.

Anh Long took a bottle of water from his pocket. Removed the top and poured a swallow between his thin lips. He stroked his killer, then spat a stream of water into its beak. The bird bokked in frustration. Shocker wore a What the Hell? expression, though the rest of us had seen this before. It was a technique to keep the birds hydrated, to improve performance. They wouldn't drink on command, too nervous around fight rings to do anything but bok, poop, and wait anxiously for the inevitable fights. *Anh Long* obviously tends his own fighters.

The boy stood with arms outstretched, and walked the rooster quickly back to the cages. The crowd around the ring chatted quietly, waiting for the Elder Dragon to return before starting the next battle.

Anh Long looked at us and smiled, *Excuse me.* He said, "Cock fighting has been in my family since its invention. It is a great source of pride, a tradition that brought villages together in the old country, and brings families together even now, in this new world. The Dragon Family values tradition." His face turned plaintive. "The Tiger Society used to, but what do they know now? Their *Anh Ho* isn't even forty years old," he said, meaning the Elder Tiger. "And they like *dog fights*, for Buddha's sake." He spat, grimacing. "They have lost touch with their roots, adopting American religion and traditions, losing their identities and respect in the process. And what are we without roots and civility?" He threw his hands up. *"Tu chang ca chon!"* showoff assholes.

He spat again. Glared at no one in particular. His voice took on a quiet passion. "The Two-Eleven and Oriental Baby Gangsters are boats without rudders, deep in a treacherous storm. Their Elders have failed them. They think the only way to power is to destroy the old ways of the

Families, and rule by an American gangster style. They weren't educated properly in our traditions of community, doing business so that everyone benefits. All they know is the strong take from the weak, and they do it with guns and cruelty. They have become the Viet Cong reincarnated." He sighed sadly. "Myself and other Elders of the Dragon Family have tried for years to be diplomatic towards the Tiger Society; we understand the cultural pressures that have influenced their direction and behavior. But we have our own Family troubles to worry about. We can't afford to put any more energy into righting their problems. And because of that, they have started *attacking* us, dismantling our nets thread by thread so that our catch becomes less while theirs grows larger."

He chopped a hand into his palm loudly, eyes wide. He focused on our attentive faces. Waved a hand at me. "No one wants war. Our people are in enough danger as it is. Can you do this without revealing us as allies?"

I glanced at my girl, at Shocker. They nodded, and I too felt we could operate under some fabricated premise, one that would allow our associates to stay in the dark. Almost immediately I had an idea.

You miss creating scams, my subconscious said, rubbing mental hands in giddy anticipation.

"No problem. Big Guns will have to lay low. We'll make sure of that."

Anh Long nodded. "I have someone who is a specialist at operating out of sight. I think he will be of help." He looked at his *Em Hung* and commanded, "Take them to see Loc. Tell my *Con Xoan* he is to give Razor and his team whatever assistance they need."

"It will be done *Anh Long*," Big Guns assured him.

Hmm. He's loaning us his Eldest Son ... that's a big deal in Asian culture, showing us and the mission the highest respect. I felt a mountain of responsibility suddenly weigh me down. It wasn't unpleasant. I do my best work under pressure, and usually show my ass when this particular feeling strikes me. Sometimes I literally show it.

My responsibilities involving people have always been minimal - my bitch and my bike were all I ever took care of. This job here has thrust a load on me I've never felt the consequence of before. I hated to admit it, but doing good for a lot of people felt sort of ... okay.

Yeah, but if you screw up people that counted on you could get hurt. Do you really want go through with this? I grilled myself, having second thoughts. *You know damn well you don't like being around so many people for very long. You could still back out, give some BS excuse ...*

"Quit trippin'," I muttered. Blondie patted my shoulder encouragingly. *Anh Long* gave me a sharp look. I told him, "You honor us. I'll do my best to hold up my end."

"You are a general about to go to war," he said gravely. "I have no doubt you will give your best effort." He looked at me, then Blondie, Shocker, knowing our reputations as accomplished fighters. He said, "War requires speed of mind and body, ruthless nature, to win. Your war council has more than enough."

The compliment had its intended effect. The girls smiled. My inner wolf howled, chest tingling, hoping for a chance to whet his muzzle on enemy blood at the nearest opportunity.

Anh Long was about to return to his cock fights when Shocker asked him, "What's your *Con Xoan's* name?"

~ ~ ~

"Loc was a sniper in the Marines," Big Guns told me as we parked by the harbor. Ace, Shocker, and Blondie pulled in next to his Prelude. He killed the ignition. Bayou mud breezed our faces as we got out. Seagulls cawed over the fishing boats docked at the piers, scavenging for scraps of decaying fish, shrimp or crabs that could be sensed on the old wooden planks. Big Guns closed his door. We did the same, gathering around him so he could brief us on the mysterious Viet killer. "Loc is not, uh, right in the head." He scratched his cheek.

"You mean he got messed up in the Iraq War?" Shocker asked, brushing a lock of hair out of her eye.

"He was messed up before he joined the military."

"What happened to him?" Blondie said.

Big Guns looked uncomfortable talking about Loc. "About ten years ago his baby died. Then his fiancé left him."

"Ouch," Ace commented. The girls' eyes widened at the juicy gossip.

"Yeah," Big Guns agreed. "Loc was a Buddhist with a Christian girlfriend - a recipe for trouble. The Two-Eleven go to church, so naturally they were enemies of the cliques that went to temple. They ran into Loc and his girl at church one day and jumped them. She was pregnant. They were beaten badly by five or six Two-Eleven, and she lost the baby at the hospital that same day. They were devastated. Loc wasn't a violent person back then, and couldn't bring himself to retaliate. It went against his beliefs. His fiancé was an Old Testament kind of girl and thought he was weak. She left him. So he joined the Marines to learn how to kill people." He shrugged. "He became a sniper. Won some shooting competitions and some awards for valor. He conquered his cowardice, but his depression turned into something psychotic. He came back last year but won't speak to anybody. Not even his own father. He lives here, on that shrimp boat."

He pointed to a fifty-foot wooden fishing vessel, dark red paint old and flaking off, wheelhouse small and crusty with tall antennas sticking up in front of the windshield. The out-rigging for the shrimp nets were drawn up like folded wings, steel tubing and pulleys well used, rust colored with a liberal coating of white 'gull droppings.

"Boss place," Shocker said sincerely.

Blondie gave her a skeptical glance. I waved for Big Guns to lead the way. "I like psycho people. Let's see if he's home."

Fifteen boat slots, all of them full of watercraft, jet skis to eighty-foot yachts, surprisingly held no people. The backwoods bayou was not known by the general public and would hold a measure of privacy a person of Loc's nature would appreciate. I realized the fugitive in the girl-beast must have noticed the same thing.

We stepped up on the dock's platform, tall marsh grass poking up between the boards, water sloshing its high tide under our feet. Fingers of wooden planks fanned out between the boats. Loc's home was docked in the last slot, stern in, bow facing the open bayou, marsh islands dotting the brackish water with tall grass and small pine trees. A single deep channel cut through the center for traffic to and from the Biloxi Bay.

As we walked onto his pier, I looked down and read the name on the stern. "Fortune of Stealth" was painted in large yellow lettering, flaked, barnacles clinging to the waterline under it.

Big Guns stepped past the first pilings and tripped over an invisible string, catching himself hard on his hands, splinters lancing his palms. *"Cac!"* he cursed, hurriedly regaining his feet.

Trip wires were a bad sign. As an outboard motor started up somewhere I turned and shoved the girls off the pier. The motor revved, the lines holding the Fortune of Stealth to the pier dropped in the water as the boat puttered away. I took a moment to speculate on the engineering involved in Loc's setup, impressed.

Seeing there was no danger, just a tripped escape alarm, I walked back to Big Guns, the girls following. "Looks like he learned quite a bit more than how to kill," I said.

"Yeah," Big Guns grumbled. Blondie handed him a tissue for his hands. He thanked her, said, "I should have known. I forgot to mention he's paranoid."

"He's a survivor," Shocker said, once again admiring Loc's home. She nudged Ace, who looked to be studying the Marine's setup as I did.

"I'd certainly have something rigged like this if I had been on *America's Most Wanted*," I told them. Ace grinned, though she frowned severely at the reminder of her infamy.

Big Guns flashed a curious chrome smile at them. Shook his head. We turned our attention to the boat once more. It turned a half-circle, fifty yards away, motor throttling down, cutting off. The wheelhouse had a small door on the portside. It opened and an incredibly fit man emerged, stepping lightly on the deck, staring at us with black expressionless eyes. *Those eyes have seen a few dead bodies*, I surmised. Loc wore black loose fitting pants, no shoes or shirt, and looked like a stunt double for Bruce Lee. His obsidian hair was shaved high and tight, skin golden brown over a chest that has done thousands of pushups. Face strong. Clean shaven. He *looked* like a bad-ass soldier.

Big Guns cupped his mouth and yelled, "Sorry to disturb you, Loc. We were sent by *Anh Long*." Loc didn't answer. Didn't blink. His hands stayed by his sides, veins in his arms visible now that the sun broke through the clouds, a bright yellow ray crossing his eyes. Big Guns glanced at us, *See? Psycho*. He yelled, "*Anh Long* wants you to help us neutralize the Two-Eleven. You are to give this team any assistance they need."

Still no response. Big Guns introduced us. "This is Razor. He's running the operation. And this is Blondie, Shocker and Ace. All very capable people. They have *Anh Long's* blessing. You must aid them and stay out of sight. The Dragon Family is behind the scenes on this one, for reasons you already know."

Loc stared, unaffected by the information, boat lifting from the excited waves chopping against it. He seemed to be part of the vessel, in perfect balance, able to anticipate the moving deck instinctively.

"Let's go. I don't think he wants to be bothered," Blondie said.

"He doesn't look like he understands," Shocker commented. "Are you sure about this guy?"

Big Guns looked at Loc warily. "Yeah. I'm sure. He understands. That's just how he is. Come on." He started walking back to the cars.

"Wait a fucking minute," I said, gesturing at the paranoid lunatic on the boat. "We need rifle support. *Anh Long* promised us his guy. Is he going to take care of business or not?"

"He will. In his own way. Come on. Let's go before we make him uncomfortable."

"Make *him* uncomfortable?" Blondie muttered, taking my arm.

I took one last look at Loc. He could hear our complaints, yet made no effort to communicate about any of it. The bastard just stared with those killer's eyes, mute.

We stood by the cars, all of us disappointed, a little uncertain now. But I had an idea to reinvigorate our team spirit. I looked around at everyone and gave my #1 Mr. Bullshit grin. "We are a sword that will defend the innocent," I intoned. Blondie rolled her eyes. Everyone else smiled. "But we are a new sword, untested in battle. Steel gets stronger through the forging process. What do you say we lunge point first into the fire?"

Shocker cracked her knuckles. "About time." Ace put a hand on her shoulder, face firmly resolved.

Big Guns' eyes danced. He gave a sly smile and said, "You guys ever been to a dog fight?"

~ ~ ~

The east end of Biloxi had an interesting clash of denizens. Whites, Asians, African-Americans and Mexicans worked in the small businesses, shops and gas stations spanning the area cornered by Highway 90 and the Biloxi Bay. They enjoyed free drinks and entertainment while gambling their earnings at the casinos lining the water. Residential neighborhoods were jotted on the map in the mix of it all. The houses were mostly medium sized, not too close together, all of them on stilts. They were owned by working-class folks with mortgages, child support and soccer games to attend. The 'hood we drove into was at least half Vietnamese.

Big Guns and Ace were in the Prelude behind us, Shocker driving the Scion like a go-cart through the narrow two-lane streets. "We'll stop here," Big Guns said in my earpiece, a near-invisible Bluetooth device. "You guys just pull up to the house like you were invited. Tell them Tran sent you."

"I got it." I repeated it to the girls, who opted to go without earpieces since all the attention will be on them. We had gone over this twice already at our apartment. The plan to get in, conceptualized by yours truly, was great, but not everyone was pleased. Shocker's disgruntled eyes and tight jaw said she didn't like the skin-tight dress and hooker role she had to play. The girls were prostitutes, and I was their pimp. We were going to crash the 211's clubhouse in a most unconventional way: Highly Trained Boxers vs. Rooty Poot Never Had a Real Job Gangsters.

In my over-confident mind, they didn't have a chance. And for some reason that should be disturbing but isn't, I'm not afraid of attacking someone that's packing a weapon. I've seen firsthand that both of these gorgeous warriors share the same commitment to the fight game.

This was going to be a lot of fun.

The green Honda turned on the street behind our destination, their job to aid in tech support and, only if absolutely necessary, back us up. We parked in front of a nice home of sky blue vinyl siding, grass too long, dry from the summer heat that had evaporated the storm as if it had never happened. The driveway and side yard were packed with cars. White, red and champagne colored Acuras, several wildly painted and bodied Hondas on big wheels and no ground clearance. A party was in progress, and we had our party masks on.

"Hookers? Really Razor? Great plan, Mister President," Shocker sassed, blowing out a breath.

I pushed my shoulders back, straightened my collar, a blue and silver Nautica button-up. "President, bitch."

She mugged me in the rear view mirror, eyes narrowed.

Blondie got out, heels ticking on the street. She smoothed her dark green leather skirt, pushed up her boobies in a matching tight vest, bronzed shoulders glowing in the sun. Hair blinding platinum. Dark sunglasses over a wicked smile. She loved role playing, and it's been a couple of years since she's been able to play a hooker. I could sense her excitement acutely. She told Shocker, "Just pretend like you're Julia Roberts in *Pretty Woman.*"

Shocker looked at her over the roof, uncomfortable in the pale red, nearly pink silk dress that made her curves jump out in all directions. His dark brown hair fell around her shoulders in thick, shiny locks, a quick Come Hither style that couldn't fail to turn heads. Her makeup was perfectly matched to her skin, facial shape, hair and dress color. I had no idea she could get so dolled up. She looked *great*. She growled, "I'm a fighter, not an actress." But she sighed resignedly, flipped her hair in annoyance, unaccustomed to anything but a ponytail, and locked the car with the fob. Stuffed the keys in her handbag.

I noticed her left arm looked tiny without the

compression sleeve, her right substantially larger. *A mechanic's arm*, I deduced. No wonder her overhand-right feels like it's thrown by a man.

Four young Viet thugs walked out to challenge us white folks. They wore baggy slacks and colorful designer shirts, big jewelry on necks, ears, wrists. An eyebrow or two pierced. They looked relatively dangerous, especially the one with the gun poking out of his waistband. The smallest of them spoke up, surprising me with his authoritative tone. "Who are you? You're not welcome here."

I put my arms around my hookers and squeezed them close, grinning like a car salesman. "Tran sent us. Thought you guys might enjoy a little flavor at your Sausage Fest."

"We have women," Little Guy said. "And we don't pay for them." His companions scowled agreement, apparently offended that I'd insinuate they had to pay for some booty.

Blondie patted my chest, walked over to the men and pulled down her shades, a dominatrix eyeing her next submissives. She purred, "Ooh, such aggression radiating from your hard little bodies. I could do a lot with that." Her heels knocked in front of them, their eyes unable to not look at her perfect legs and butt. Little Guy licked his lips. Like a lioness spotting the weakest of the herd Blondie turned on him, her energy magnetic, sucking in his will. She towered over him, tan boobies peeking out of her vest, right in his face. "I bet you've never had a woman before, have you? You said you 'have women,' but they're just girls, aren't they?"

She stroked a finger under his chin, brushed his forearm, making his face glow and arm hair stand erect, touching areas she knew connected to parts of the brain associated with trust and reward. He moaned slightly, intoxicated by her appearance, voice and scent. She leaned down and breathed her sweet breath in Little Guy's face, voice husky, in full Seduction mode. *"You want me?"*

"Mmm-uhm," he answered, face flushed with

disorientation. He eased a hand in his pocket, grabbing his hardened dick to keep it from poking his pants out. I literally bit my tongue to fight laughter. She did that to me all the time. I was no stranger to pocket pool.

"We'll see you boys inside," Blondie said in a tone that was more imperative than declarative. She gave Little Guy's butt a pinch, pushed them out of the way, and I took my hookers' hands, smiling, Blondie leading us up the cement path that accessed the porch and front door.

The living room was dark, two couches and three chairs overfilled with teenage couples, all of them Vietnamese, girls sitting or lying on their current boyfriends, hip-hop casual the dress flavor for their clique. Techno trance laced the marijuana clouded air with wild cadences of sound, drums and trippy electronica tweaking senses as a hot-voiced female sang in an Asian tongue I didn't understand.

The little Viet hotties in the room saw Blondie and Shocker and stiffened. Their petite, cute faces made all range of emotions, mouths open in brow-furrowing envy at their legs, shoulders, long gorgeous hair and bangin' outfits. Their statuesque height. I looked at them and mimed their expressions, squeezing the source of their awe. Blondie and Shocker both pinched the *motherfuck* out of my hands, so I let go of their asses, smiled away the pain.

You'll pay for that later, my Johnson shrunk in dismay.

One of the men sitting by the hallway jumped up and ran out of the room. By the look on his face and most everyone else in the room, I'd say he was peaking on some quality ecstasy and his stomach was in rebellion. I looked at the front door as Shocker was about to close it. The guys Blondie worked her magic on had shook off the spell and were following us into the house. *Good. We need them all in the same place.*

In the kitchen an older Vietnamese woman cooked a large stir-fry meal on some kind of gas stove, pans on every burner. Bowls and long spoons took up the small counter to her left. We walked past her and she yammered something that had a greeting/excuse me inflection. An open door showed a garage with a pool table, two dozen people packed around it, stacks of cash and random jewelry on the green felt as dice rolled and the gamblers crowed. Rap music pumped from surround-sound speakers.

"Cause we smoke that Kush / and we ball like swush," Lil' Wayne flowed. The men were laughing uproariously at one man's antics over losing, a dramatic, drunken, funny show as only Asian men can do.

A stuttering hush came over them when they noticed the world-class ass walk into the room.

Blondie took point, put a hand on her poked out hip, weight on one stiletto. She pulled her shades low so she could look down her nose at everyone, assume a position of authority. They instinctively recognized her alpha status and couldn't help reacting to it. She controlled the room with her *presence*. "The enemy is in the house," her sultry voice purred, announcing the literal truth while making her audience feel sexy.

A few nervous laughs, one guy tittering like a drunk bimbo. My greasy car salesman smile stayed in place with no effort. Shocker just stood there, in neither Hooker nor Seductress mode, though still managed to emanate Boss Bitch. Men were eyeing her with wary lust and awe as well.

Blondie pushed her glasses up, then took her time walking around the table, rubbing her hands suggestively along guys' stomachs, pulling their shirts up slightly in front or back. Tousling their hair with playful feminine sounds. Every single one she touched reached for her. She moved through their groping hands with practiced ease while the girlfriends squawked like adorable, pissed off chipmunks. Shocker watched my girl with a grudging admiration.

Blondie: 2. Shocker: 1

Most of the guys were in their early twenties. All were seasoned in gangster life. That meant they would fight with or without weapons. So far, Blondie had found two more guns, making it three known on the men. No telling how many were in the house. If things went as planned, our enemy wouldn't get a chance to arm themselves.

Blondie made her way along the dice game to the last guy, rubbing his shoulders, brushing the front of his waist with the back of her hand, the outline of an automatic briefly forming on his rayon shirt. *Four guns,* I considered. *Wonder how many are at the fight ring???*

I turned to look at the ends of the garage. The bay door was wide open on the driveway thirty feet away, shelves with boxes lining the walls, lawn equipment circling a riding mower in front of two tricked Acuras. My head spun to look at the other end. A door was open onto the backyard. A wide, green lawn and chain link fence looked picturesque through the frame. Blondie indicated that her charms were inseminated in the men and we could move on to the next group.

We walked outside. The sun was warm and the air was loud. Bass thundered from woofers on the patio deck, fast, hard-core rap that encouraged everyone to push a motherfucker, hit a motherfucker.

Ah ... LOVE it when the music fits the scene!

"We see you," Big Guns said in my ear. I glanced around, beyond the fence. Houses flanked us. The one behind had a large shed on the far side of its yard, fifty yards away. Several fig trees provided cover for Big Guns and Ace, who crouched among the thick foliage with an EMP emitter, a device about the size of a large boom box. It transmitted powerful electromagnetic pulses out of its plastic, rectangular antenna. What looked like golf ball-type dimples textured its face. With a rechargeable 24 volt cell, it only weighed twelve pounds. My girl built it to shut down cars, computers, cell phones – police stations-anything electronically dependent. They're easier to construct than you'd think. You can't imagine how handy the thing was when we were crooks.

"Turn it on in ten second intervals when the action starts," I murmured. That would kill their phones and cars, while allowing us to communicate every sixth of a minute if we needed to. They wouldn't be able to call any backup, or flee from us in their cars. We had to take care of business before they realized they were trapped; people fight much harder when they see they have no escape. But I wasn't worried about blundering. I have experience attacking crowds like this. And the girls had a special treat up their skirts for them.

The dog fight looked much like the cock fight we had seen earlier, only the ring was four feet tall and there were no children or older people present. The thugs emoted their pleasure or frustration in a mix of English and Vietnamese. Two white girls, both petite brunettes in jeans and bikini tops, stood out among them, long-lashed eyes widening at the show stopping hookers encroaching on their territory. Blondie and Shocker ignored their baleful looks, focusing on the guys that screamed raucously around the snarling dogs in the ring, two red-nose pit bulls tearing at each other's necks, legs and haunches in wet brown dirt.

The brutality of the animals had ignited all sorts of special primal feelings in the men, warrior genes demanding for the tribe to hunt, kill, feel pleasure at dominating lesser animals. They cheered for blood, for money and status, excited anxiously and carnally. The atmosphere was more raw than the cock fight had been, of more consequence. The morally conscious would say this exciting action was wrong, even more so than the cock fighting. Dogs are man's best friend, bluh, bluh, while we eat chicken. However you want to use cultural or religious values to justify your eating or fighting of other species is your business. I have no moral ambiguity on the issue. Animals share equal rights in my eyes. I eat chicken, and I'll eat your dog if you get me mad enough.

Playing my role was all about the greasy smile. These people believed the pimp act with no trouble. I was able to invade their space without slapping or sweet talking anyone. Who wants to talk to a greasy pimp? My assumed title gave me freedom from having to socialize. "Genius," I muttered in appreciation to my brain, feeling a deserved moment of ego.

Pimp smooth, I slid a hand over my greased back hair.

"They look too absorbed by the dogs. How are we going to play this?" Shocker whispered flirtatiously in my ear, smiling and stroking my cheek.

I brushed my lips on her ear. She giggled. I said, "You have the Special K?"

"Mmm-hmm." She smiled and cut her eyes at some guy checking her out. Waved playfully.

"Follow Blondie's lead."

"Okay," she grumbled, then hurriedly planted the hooker smile on again.

I walked over and squeezed my girl's butt. I do that a lot, so much that it's become a part of our communication. This squeeze said, *Get to work, woman.*

"Gotcha, Raz," she responded, inclining her head at Shocker. They couldn't walk in the grass around the fight ring in heels and maintain the body language they wished to project. But there were brick and stone walkways throughout the yard, and the deck was large, the width of the house, the benches filled with people, all of them drinking beer or mixed drinks from a makeshift bar, a small table lined with booze and two hotties in bikinis, a cooler of ice and a keg of beer between them on the stained wood.

My hookers walked on the brick path to the fight ring

like runway models, hair, boobies and buttocks bouncing in eye pleasing fashion. The dog fighters noticed the bombshells and amped up their boisterous play. With testosterone levels pegged to the max from the vicious fights, their sex drives were accelerated as well. The jump from Fight to Fuck was an easy matter for any man of thug/gangster breed. The Gorgeous Woman Effect will make a man do really stupid things, so I wasn't surprised to hear men shout loud, ridiculous bets, flashing wads of cash while their eyes were glued to Blondie and Shocker. Some were so drunk or hormonally crazed they were imitating the dogs, barking, snarling, heads whipping back and forth as if they were worrying an enemy's hide. My inner wolf responded, dosing me with a quaking surge of adrenaline and endorphin's. I howled a challenge.

With their goal of riveting attention accomplished, the hookers spun on the runway and strutted over to the deck, stepping up by the girls who poured Bud Light in plastic cups from the ice cold keg, drops of condensation twinkling wetly on the stainless steel. No one paid me any attention, so I sat in a lawn chair, kicked back to watch the show.

"Thank you ladies," Blondie told the pretty, scowling girls. "You've done great. You can leave now." She flicked a dismissive hand, and the girls shuffled aside with intimidated disbelief, shamefully walked off the deck into the house.

"Ha!" I clapped. "Status superseded." I dug out my cocaine. Took a few quick bumps.

Blondie looked over at the fight ring. Every eye was on the new bartenders – the guys from the porch, the dicers from the garage, the thugs at the fight ring – they all stared at the baddest white girls they've ever seen. Blondie had their attention, but it wasn't enough. She needed to bring everyone together. She looked at Shocker. "Ever done a keg stand?"

"Um..."

"Never mind. Just hold up my legs." She turned to the nearest gangster, Little Guy, and curled a finger at him. He grinned like a lottery winner, stepped closer to the goddesses and the keg between them. "Hold the tap to my mouth and count the seconds," Blondie demanded. Little Guy nodded rapidly. Blondie smiled at the crowd and announced, "There's a new bar service on the scene. Any of you weak motherfuckers care to challenge me in a keg stand?"

The men raised their drinks or shouted in Vietnamese, English, some lewd comments in French.

A line began forming at the bar. Blondie grabbed the keg's rim with both hands and jumped into a handstand, long legs stabbing into the air, stilettos tipping her magnificence like lightning rods on a skyscraper. Shocker grabbed her calves, held her with a small feminine grunt, the sound more annoyance than strain. Their arms bulged with ripped muscle, and eyes widened in amazement. I could see the wheels turning in the marks' heads. *How can prostitutes look like this?* their mystified faces said.

Blondie's skirt rode down enough so that everyone got to see her bright green panties and any questions they may have had about her being a hooker were forgotten.

She shows everyone but me, I pouted to myself.

A supermodel hooker doing a keg stand panties flash was quite the spectacle. Blondie had drugged everyone with lust or envy, emotions that would blind them from catching on to the next phase of our job: drugging them for real.

Blondie sucked the tap in Little Guy's hand while he counted out the seconds. The men surrounding them bellowed, "Go! Go! Go!" while girlfriends stood on the outskirts with pure hatred coloring their lovely epicanthic eyes. Blondie spat out the tap after a full minute and screamed, "Suck it! You worms can't beat that!"

Laughing genuinely for the first time since we arrived, Shocker lowered her. No one wanted to attempt a keg stand, likely fearing the ridicule they would suffer when they failed to beat Blondie. My girl straightened her clothes, *hmmpted* in satisfaction, looked over at me.

I mouthed "green" and snorted a wonderful drip, lacing my fingers behind my head.

The girls began filling cups of beer, the drink suddenly more popular. As I pondered my girl's success as a top-rate Budweiser spokes model, I watched her and Shocker slip Ketamine into over twenty cups of brew. The recipients slurped it up happily, wiping cold foam from mouths that continually vied for the attention of the goddesses running the show.

I chuckled, clapped my hands, then broke out the coke once more. The lawn chair was comfy. I lay it all the way back. Crossed my ankles. Snorted several gigantic bumps.

The tranquilizer took effect almost immediately. The guys were draining their cups quickly to have a reason to get closer to the girls again, getting refills and more Special K. They were staggering around after the first cup, and sitting down after the second. Some of the girlfriends were tending their inebriated men with great suspicion, though I think they believed their men were simply swooning under Blondie's and Shocker's influence.

That's what they want to believe, I smirked in thought. The guys, and most of the girls, had been drinking for hours before we got here. The Ketamine wouldn't be noticed by these people until it was too late.

The sun felt great heating my face and arms. Being a greasy pimp at a house party, I felt obliged to unbutton my shirt, pull it open so everyone could admire or hate on my greasy abs. I laid back again, waiting for Blondie to tell me our marks were ready for the *coup de grâce*.

"Are you ready yet?" Big Guns said in my ear. "You

could have annihilated them after B flashed her junk."

I laughed, murmured, "This is her game. She'll tell us when it's our turn to play."

He sighed in response, and I pictured his teeth flashing silver impatience. He had wanted to be in the mix of things. His hands-on attitude is what made me respect the gang leader when I first met him, five or six years ago. He never ordered his men to do anything he wouldn't do himself. He had many standards as a crew leader I'd do well to observe.

I can't remember the last time I've seen a keg empty as fast as this one did. After thirty minutes nearly every man present was plastered on alcohol, and unknowingly plastered on something that's not supposed to be consumed with alcohol. Two people were vomiting out by the fence. Another was sound asleep on his back, wide nose casting a shadow on his chin, bright sun baking his skin. The dogs were completely forgotten about, three of them tied to the fence. One licked up a puddle of puke. Others ran around trailing leashes. Blondie and Shocker were having to be more aggressive in fending off advances as men lost further control.

I sensed the critical mass on the horizon and stood. Took my shirt off. Blondie gave me a nod, pivoting away from groping hands. Big Guns said, "EMP is on," and I walked over to the deck, stepped up, walked with purpose to a bench lining the middle of the handrail. Shoved the people sitting on it out of my way and stood atop it, turning to face the crowd that finally took serious note of me. The people I had ejected cried foul. Those sitting or lying sensed something was wrong and began standing. I paid them no attention, held up my hands.

"Silence, peasants!" I roared, commanding voice ensnaring everyone. Vietnamese didn't like being called peasants. I had their undivided attention. I projected my words, aiming to sound like a passionate Supreme Court judge. "The Two-Eleven and Oriental Baby Gangsters are hereby stripped of their holdings and shall cease all operations on the Coast. You have offended and hurt hundreds of people you had no business molesting, and the People will no longer stand for it. We are here to represent the people's interest."

I caught Blondie rolling her eyes. *Damn you're fried on coke*, Shocker pooh-pooh faced me.

I snorted, eyes darting, heart racing with the thrill. *I'd make a swell judge.*

While everyone watched me, Blondie and Shocker had taken off their heels, pulled some flats from their handbags and slipped them on. Put the stilettos in the bags. Dropped them on a bench. Put hair in ponytails. Shocker had brass knuckles over black leather gloves. Blondie pulled on a pair of similar gloves and gripped two iron bars, each as big as a roll of quarters.

I flexed my bare fists. Calmly, in no hurry, I took a set of bouncer gloves from a pocket. Took my sweet time putting them on. I held my weapons out for silence and was rewarded with dozens of glaring eyes. Judge Razor sentenced them. "Today you will be punished for what you've done. If you choose to continue on your ignoble course, as I'm sure you will, we'll be back. And we'll come back as many times as it takes for you idiots to get the message."

"What are you a fed? Fuck you *and* those undercover hoes!" Little Guy raged at me, finger aimed accusingly at my team members, slurring, unbalanced. Mad as hell because he had been teased like a common mark at a titty bar. "We are forty strong, and can have more with a phone call. How you think you can punish us?"

For an answer, I casually kicked him in the face. My size 12 Rockport bludgeoned his fragile cheekbone from my elevated position. "Aaarrrgh!" he gasped, flailing at the people around him to keep from going down. They caught him, eyeing me with a hilarious, lethargic surprise. Not only had I assaulted their Brother, I had threatened their way of life. They screamed drunken-drugged battle cries and pushed each other out of the way to get at me.

I jumped off the bench, over the handrail to the grass, landing on balance. Looked up to see Blondie and Shocker wade into the crowd with fast, devastating punches, all business, taking advantage of the attention on me to hit them in the back of their heads, brutal rabbit punches dropping the tranquilized men with ease. They moved quickly toward the men with guns and knocked them senseless before the marks even knew a fight was happening.

A flurry of arms and grim faces came at me from the left, more jumping the handrail, four guys trying to encircle me. I danced out of their trap, popping long jabs into their enraged eyes. I planted my back foot, pushed off it hard and threw a right-hand into the chin of the closest man. It was a bone-jarring blow, felt deep in my shoulder. His jaw broke in more than one place, he hit the grass on his stomach, groaning dully, unconscious. The other three saw the ease and precision with which I had dispatched their comrade and sobered.

They slowed their charge, but that didn't help; I charged *them*, the unexpected *blitzkrieg* freezing them long enough for me to pump my legs, hips, roll shoulders, uppercuts dropping two, a quick pivot and overhand-right taking out the third. My tightened fists went through them like hydraulic shafts, pistoning with explosive, endless energy, thwacking them to the ground. Their drugged equilibriums had no luck against my speed. I looked around and saw witnesses staring at me, hesitant to fight the killer wolf. Several fled as fast as they could, staggering, leaping bodies on the lawn and deck, crashing through the house as

Blondie's iron-barred fists blazed in their wake. Others jumped the fence, taking refuge in neighboring yards. A pit bull attacked one of the fence leapers, giving in to his instinct to chase and bite things that ran. The guy screamed in pain, pants tearing loudly, flesh gouged from sharp canines.

"Ha!" I clapped.

I turned and ran around the deck to the opposite side of my hookers to block people escaping their fury. There were at least a dozen thugs and two Viet girls still fighting, packed together, facing the blistering combos of the girl-beast and blonde warrior. With no room to swing without hitting each other they were slowly pushed back and off the deck. One spotted me coming up behind them and shouted a warning. "*Can than!*"

I stepped up swiftly and leaped, bringing my knee into a random face. His nose felt gruesome breaking under my patella. I threw an uppercut at the same time, smashing his eye. He cried out in agony and blood slicked under my boots. Several turned and swung wild, desperate, panicked punches. I ducked my head back quickly, hitting someone's face behind me. A fist cracked against my ear, rocking my head. The blow connected cleanly, but only served to sharpen my focus.

"Good shot," I told the man, drilling him with a jab, right-hand, left-hook combo. He whooshed out a breath as his stomach received the hook, sinking to his knees.

More punches rained on me, four, five, six guys, as I turned back around, hands up, slapping fists aside, weaving head, able to see the amateur punches coming, focusing on slick movement to avoid clean hits. Fortunately these guys weren't in top form at present and couldn't muster enough strength to hit very hard. And there's just such a huge difference in skill between professionally trained fighters and average street gangsters. I held a significant height and reach advantage over them, as well, and used it to keep them on the end of my punches, away from me.

My arms felt like they could go for hours, the excitement of the battle imbibing my muscles with limitless fuel. I started throwing long, straight, quick punches, combos with buzz saw effect. A line of men seven feet wide tried to press in on me, bold now that they were cornered. I focused peripherally on any that jumped too far over the line I mentally drew on the deck, eyes extremely wide, watching everything at once. I pivoted on them smoothly and struck, lighting them up with hard, furious shots, turning to hit another with explosive speed, busting lips, eyes, blood flowering on faces, resetting shoulders to relax and recover a fraction of a second before throwing hard again. They had no idea how to get close to me, the confines of the deck holding them together, preventing them from surrounding me, getting inside my punches. None of them were even close to being on my level. I was a wolf among medium sized doggies, and they knew it.

To be a good sport – and make it more of a challenge – I decided to use just my left-hook. Every fighter has a punch they really excel at. Blondie had a great jab, long, crisp, and on time – she could knock a man down with it, without an iron bar. Shocker had an inhuman overhand-right. My punch was the hook. I could throw it from any angle, incredibly fast, in a Roy Jones, Jr. style.

A guy with a map of Vietnam on his shirt lunged at me with a looping punch. I leaned to the side, weight over my left foot, exploding off it to throw a hook into his cheek. *Crunch!* My fist resounded. He squinted hard as the blow displaced his face in space-time, throwing an unconscious punch on the way to the ground. His fist brushed my leg.

I pivoted to the left, right, slapping aside several swings of a wooden stick that scattered my foes. An older woman holding a thick broom, the cook that greeted us on the way in, thrashed it insanely, hard wood cracking into faces and necks on either side as she screamed in Vietnamese. It was straight out of a comedy movie.

I was reluctant to hit the woman, especially since she was helping me. Several men she had smacked yelled at her. She realized what she was doing, adjusted her grip on the stick and made to spear me with it. I smiled at her, *Come on, really?* Her face scrunched up for a war cry, then distorted gruesomely as Shocker's brass knuckles caved in her cheek, smashing jaw, teeth. She dropped, limp, trampled on by two men scrambling to avoid the girl-beast's devastating metal fists.

"*Haaa!*" I clapped. Snorted a drip, then ran headlong into the melee, meeting my warrior hookers in the center, the three of us clearing the deck with our preferred punches, men running away hurt, girls crying shrilly, curses, pleas, questions shouted desperately in rapid Vietnamese. It was chaos, and I reveled in the collective panic of the fleeing enemy. "Bitch!" I shouted, slugging an overweight thug that deigned to challenge my position as King of the Deck.

With no targets to seek and destroy, I inspected Blondie and the girl-beast. My girl's vest and skirt were twisted on her curves, hair wild, lip leaking blood from a corner. She licked it, giving a wicked smile. The Shocker had a wardrobe malfunction, one bra-clad boobie sticking out, bright white, blood spotted in the sun, torn strap hanging. She still wore her Fight mode face: brows low and tight, eyes dark and lips peeled back from her gritted teeth. Two long scratches on her cheek. I looked down. Her brass knuckles glistened red in her shadow. Veins throbbed in her freaky arms. She couldn't wait to hit something else.

She pulsed an energy I was envious of. She was a true berserker, a rare human being, her physical abilities able to defy nature. What little I was able to watch of her work was a real pleasure. *Damn. I should've had Big Guns film this.*

Noticing my interest was more intent on the girl-beast than her, Blondie folded her arms and glowered. I'm usually all over her after a job like this. And it's been a long time since we've done a job. Before I could explain my leering was out of respect, Big Guns refocused our attention on the not-quite-finished job at hand.

"Trouble," he said in my ear.

I froze. "Where?"

"Two cars pulled up. Doesn't look like a mob."

"It couldn't be. The EMP prevented anyone from calling for help." There are probably a dozen people out front wondering why their phones and cars won't work.

"There must have been a meeting scheduled. Diep just got out of one car. What's he doing here?" he muttered in thought. "Four guys got out of the other car. His personal guard. They are a little more capable than the *lons* you put to sleep. Be careful."

"All right." I looked at the girls. "Party's not over yet."

"How many?" Blondie said.

"Five. One is Diep."

Blondie's eyes popped.

"Who's that?" Shocker said. Her demeanor was completely different now. More human.

"He runs the Tiger Society," Blondie breathed, mentally floored as the ramifications dawned on her. "What the fuck???" She took a breath, composed her hair.

"I'm not sure why he's here and the Two-Eleven and OBG bosses aren't. And I don't care. This is an opportunity to grab the snake by the head." I swung my arms to prevent stiffness.

Shocker tapped her fists together. *Clang.* "Let's get them before I cool down."

My envy betrayed me again as the girl-beast marched over and punched a guy that was trying to get up. He exhaled sharply as the blow hit behind his ear, knocking his head back to the deck, asleep. Blondie glared at me, fuming, and I realized I should have at least complimented the way her ass looked during the fight before she spun on a toe and stalked away to the kitchen entrance, standing to one side.

I sighed, looked around the yard. Several dogs were sniffing the men on the ground. The one still alive in the ring was trying to leap the wooden wall, limping around with his long pink tongue wagging, too injured to make the jump. Several wads of cash and baggies of drugs were in the grass. The stereo and speakers on the deck were destroyed and scattered, beer bottles and cups and knocked out Special K victims lay strewn everywhere. The tranquilizer had definitely supplemented our fist work. If it wasn't so damn smart it would feel like cheating. I inhaled with a deep sense of achievement.

I walked to the kitchen door. The girls stood on the sides, out of sight of anyone inside. Diep and his crew spotted me as soon as they walked into the kitchen. Through the sliding glass door I saw several girls and Little Guy all talking at once and gesturing at the backyard. Diep barked an order. Little Guy ushered the girls into the living room quickly, heads down, and four stocky men surrounded their boss like shields, one drawing a gun from a shoulder holster.

"Shit. Gun." I told my crew. Big Guns groaned. I looked at Blondie, Shocker. "Five guys, one known gun. What do you want to do?"

"Shit, babe. Fuck them up." Blondie flexed her leather fists around the iron bars.

Shocker looked at me, eyes of a demon, in Fight mode once again. She growled, "They won't be quick enough. Let them get close."

Oh, man! Was this chick beyond awesome or what?

I nodded, put on my greasy, hate-me-pimp-face, and

yelled, "Hey Diep! You fucking peasant. *Lon,*" pussy. "Your boys throw a shitty party, man. They couldn't even handle a little S and M action from two hookers."

Blondie groaned in exasperation. Shocker directed her beastly eyes at me. I gave them a greasy car salesman smile, then watched Diep and his boys rush out the door to confront me.

The leader of the Tiger Society was small framed but tall for a Vietnamese. He looked very American. His hair was cut in a preppy style, mustache and goatee trimmed low on a lean, tawny face. Eyes too close together, giving him a mean countenance. Dress slacks, black silk shirt. His presence said C*hief,* and he gave me the feeling his rep for cruelty wasn't exaggerated. He pointed a finger at me, angry. "Who - " he started, freezing at the sight of the carnage.

The pause was all the girls needed. Blondie announced her presence with a hook thrown into the crotch of the gunman, instantly grabbing and wrestling the pistol from his hands. She leaned back then forward quickly, hammering the weapon into his stomach and head repeatedly. He folded under her vicious assault.

Shocker said hello with two loaded, huge right-hands back to back, WHAM! WHAM! pulverizing the heads of the two closest to her. They went down awkwardly and she kept hitting them, arms churning out serious hurt with every thudding shot.

Blondie aimed the gun at the remaining bodyguard, who was trying to pull a gun from behind his back. "Don't do it," she warned, pointing the muzzle at his eyes. He made a frustrated sound of anger, held his hands up reluctantly. Shocker clocked him in the back of the head, stumbling as he fell against her.

In the seven seconds it took for this to take place, Diep had turned to see his men being attacked, turned back to see me start after him. He pulled a gun from under his shirt and managed to get behind Shocker as she tussled and dropped the bodyguard. He grabbed her around the shoulders, put the gun to her head. She stilled, eyes bugging, and a most distressing and unexpected emotion crossed her features: fear.

She's been shot before.

Diep screamed at us, a cornered animal. "I'll shoot her! Get away! I'll splatter her brain - "

His hand holding the gun exploded in a red spray, the bullet going through his palm, into the vinyl siding he slumped against. Blood, skin and bits of metacarpals coated Shocker's hair, cheek, arm and dress, dripped on the ground. The gun clattered on the patio. Diep roared in agony, voice high, ululating. He clutched his wrist in an attempt to tourniquet the flow of arterial blood skeeting everywhere. He leaned against the house, eyes rolling wildly from the trauma, whimpering, then screaming, calling out names to come help.

Shocker decided to be of assistance. He looked up at her. She zeroed in on his raised chin and sent her brass hook on a bombing mission, grunting with animalistic femininity as it knocked him out of his misery. He slid down the wall, fell on his side, face on cement. His pain quiet, we could hear the sounds of summer in the neighborhood, the faint techno still beating in the living room. Shocker leaned down and took the belt off a bodyguard, looped it around Diep's wrist tightly and sat him up. Raised his injured arm over and behind his head, leaving it there. "It's above his heart. He won't bleed to death before the EMTs get here," she said, trying to wipe blood off her face. It just smeared like war paint, the sight and smell causing all kinds of weird sensations in my mouth. I wanted to *bite* something.

"Who shot him?" Blondie said, looking out over the fence in the direction it had been fired from. "Did Big G bring a rifle?"

"No," I replied, knowing who gave us sniper support. I shielded my eyes, searching the roof tops of the many houses visible on the next block. The shingles were bright with afternoon light. One home over a hundred yards away had a chimney with a figure dressed in black lying on the side of it. A huge black rifle on a tripod was propped in front of him, silenced, I assumed, since we never heard the shot. I could feel the cross-hairs as he surveyed us with his scope. I help up a hand, flashed an OK in appreciation.

Blondie saw him, too. "Who the freak is that?"

"Loc," Shocker breathed.

I grinned broadly, pleased with my team. "Our new recruit."

VI. I#@k That

I squatted down behind my girl and said to her ass, "Good job!" I high-fived her cakes before she could scoot out of the way, grinning at her yelp. I ducked back from her responding swing.

"Fucker! And just when I was about to show you another of Victoria's Secrets." She folded her arms, turned her head away.

We stood in our apartment bedroom. Blondie wore a large white towel wrapped around her, a smaller one on her head. She smelled like exotic bath oils. I was naked. I sat on the bed, took my socks off. "Sorry Babe. You know I can't help myself. Your ass did such a masterful job mesmerizing all those gangsters, I just had to give kudos."

"Mmm-hmm, right." The setting sun beamed its rays through the huge window behind her. Tie-dyed hues played artfully on her face and white shrouded curves. She smiled forgiveness. "All right then. Go take your shower. I'll be ready when you get out." She ran a hand down my chest, stomach, and flicked a finger at the head of my penis.

Ow! my Johnson complained happily. I resisted the urge to take her right then, and padded quickly to the shower, ignoring the meat-seeking missile slapping my legs as if to try and turn me around.

Clean, dry, with a pair of black boxer-briefs on, I walked back into our bedroom. The space was large and welcoming. The carpet was blue, walls a simple white with several motorcycle and boxing scenes painted directly on the sheetrock in one corner. The opposite side of the room was one of my masterpieces (if I do say so). Airbrushed in realistic style was a field of flowers, grass tall up close, shorter in the background. Walking in the middle of the field were three very primitive, very naked women. Blonde. Brunette. Scarlet. Raw gorgeous, no makeup or expensive hair styles. No jewelry. Their beauty was in the most natural state, without any possibility of shallowness. When I viewed them I felt refreshed. When I asked my roommate what she thought she waggled her hand to indicate mediocrity and said, "Aaa..."

The head of the bed was positioned right under them, facing the window, white sheets glowing the same golden red as the hair of my scarlet fantasy girl, a magical nest for the real goddess sprawled in the middle on top of several pillows. Legs crossed at the ankles, tall black boots ending mid-thigh. A lacy garter of some material I didn't know but instantly liked was clipped to them. Her lingerie was purple and light green, lacy white around her boobies. Cute little darker green bows topped her shoulders, more in her hair, which was almost dry now, long locks framing her makeup-less face. My eyes moved down. Her stomach was bare and mouth-watering. She rubbed her hands along her sides, over her stomach, slowly, sensuously, eyes half closed. She wasn't acting now; this was the real Blondie. The woman that loved me. Her manner was completely different than when she was working her charms on marks. Her sincere, vulnerable seduction was just for me, really special, and *much* hotter.

She opened her eyes and said in a tender, breathy voice, "You like?"

"Oh. Yeah." I got onto the foot of the bed, on my knees, started rubbing her boots.

She chortled in pleasure. "Well, you chewed up the last lingerie I bought - you still owe me for that, by the way - so I decided to go a different route this time."

"Different? How could you possibly look any sexier?"

For an answer, she opened her legs, showing me the

sexiest pair of crotch-less panties on Earth, a purple see-through garment that showcased her blonde pubbies like jewelry at Zales. My erection was borderline painful. She saw my other brain trying to take the controls and put a boot on my chest, pushed me back, smiling slyly. *You owe me mega foreplay* her beautiful eyes narrowed at me.

I held my hands up. "Hey. If your kitty cat did *that* to those panties, I'm not going anywhere near that thing."

She laughed loudly. "Yeah right." She put her legs under her quickly, sat up on her knees, mouth an inch from mine, bright eyes staring into me. She stroked the front of my underwear, whispering, "You'll go near 'that thing' when I say so. Understand?"

All I could do was moan in response.

~ ~ ~

"I've been waiting out here forever," Shocker complained as Blondie let her in the front door. "I saw your lights blinking on and off real fast, and I heard music, so I knew you were here. What the hell?"

"We have a Clapper," I elaborated, sitting in a chair in the living room.

Blondie bit her lip, closed the door.

"A Clapper? So you two just hang out and clap your hands to music?"

"Yeah. Let's say we were clapping our hands." I smiled facetiously.

Blondie cleared her throat, fighting a grin.

It dawned on Shocker what was making the lights blink as if a stoned lab monkey were in control of the switch. She sighed, shook her head. "You freaks have so much sex you make *me* want to take a pregnancy test."

"Where's Ace?" Blondie said, sitting on a gray leather divan that matched my chair, a small glass table between us, lamp on, illuminating her fresh glow of makeup. The room had a low ceiling to give a feeling of closeness, hardwood floor, no rugs, a small TV that we never used. The art on the walls was a mix of weirdness. Our tastes in paintings went from gruesome evil to breathtaking landscapes and a Marilyn Monroe portrait. We had a shitload of art all over the apartment.

Shocker inspected the seat next to Blondie before sitting on it hesitantly. "Ace is at Bobby's house. No telling what they're up to. Perry will be here in a few minutes. He's going to cook us a big meal." She smiled fondly, adjusting her snug fitting tank, the power source for her silky black compression sleeve. "Any news from Big Guns?"

I looked at Blondie. She said to Shocker, "Right after we crashed the Two-Eleven's party Diep went to the hospital, where an army of gangsters showed up. Biloxi PD had to make them leave. The entire Tiger Society has been alerted, nationwide. Big G said every TS affiliate old enough to hold a weapon has been armed and given our descriptions."

"Good," Shocker smiled. "I don't mind being recognized in this instance."

I laughed. "Next time we're filming it."

"When is the next time, Mister President?" They both looked at me, but before I could answer someone knocked on the door.

"I got it." Blondie padded barefoot to the door, yellow shorts and white blouse seeming to make her hair brighter. She peeped through the hole, squealed in delight and jerked the door open, arms wide to give Perry a hug. Bobby and Ace crowded behind him, all smiles.

Perry walked into her arms, hands full of grocery bags, Tupperware. "Sweetheart," he greeted her.

She squeezed around his shoulders with dainty cuteness, stepped back, waved everyone in and closed it. Pointed to the kitchen, the living room. "Make yourselves at home."

Perry nodded to Shocker, who stood to hug him quickly.

Nodded to me, bags crinkling in his huge hands. "I heard you guys had quite a day. Thought I'd help replenish those weapons you call arms and legs." He grinned, walked into the kitchen, Blondie following.

I looked at Shocker. "What a swell guy."

She smiled. "You won't say that after he swells your gut with all the food he's going to spoil us with."

"True." I patted my stomach. It gave a slight growl, reacting to the sublime smell I knew would be wafting from my kitchen any minute.

Ace leaned over and kissed Shocker. "Dear," he said endearingly. I squinted at his shirt. WIRED was proclaimed in artfully colored wires and electronic components.

"Hey you. What you have two been working on?" she said, smiling *Hello* to Bobby.

Big Swoll answered. "Wrecking." He stood in front of the TV facing us, hands in jeans pockets, another bodybuilder tank top showing off his immensity, this one fluorescent orange.

"Ace, you said before that you have a 'Wrecker.' I'm not as computer savvy as you and Blondie. Care to explain what that is?" I queried.

"He's Apex," Blondie said as Ace opened his mouth. She licked something off her finger, walking out of the kitchen.

Ace never closed his mouth, staring at her incredulously. "How..."

Blondie smiled at him. Turned to me. "Remember when we read about botnets?"

I nodded. "A supercomputer comprised of millions of connected PCs and laptops."

Blondie's eyes gleamed. "It's beyond my experience, though I've always wanted to design malware to get a system like that going."

"No you don't," Ace muttered, staring at the carpet.

My girl shrugged. "Botnets start with creating a Trojan

virus inside a 'free download' ad." She didn't let his cynical attitude affect her excitement. "Email it to a gazillion people and sit back and count how many marks click on it. You'll have control of their computer's processing power. Take over a few million computers and you'll have more processing capability than the world's best supercomputers." She smiled wistfully. "There are only a few known botnets. The people running them sometimes lease processing time, similar to how a university rents time on their supercomputers. I needed some major mojo for a job in 0-nine, and found a notorious operator on the 'Net that called himself Apex. I tried to trace his location but couldn't, of course." Her hands typed an air keyboard while her face looked adorable in disappointment. Then she smiled, *No prob.* "But I was able to find other chat rooms he did business in. 'Wrecker' and 'Wrecking' were how he described his rig and work."

"You're Barbie Killer?" Ace said, voice still tinged with disbelief, though now full of respect.

"Recognize, motherfucker." Blondie smiled prettily, held her fist out. He bumped it and gave a nervous grin, turned to his girl.

Shocker and I frowned at each other. Bobby *hmmed* thoughtfully. Perry, oblivious to us, sang a country song while pans sizzled and spices filled the air-conditioned apartment.

"I get the Barbie Killer tag," Shocker said, inclining her head at my girl. She looked at Ace, deciding whether to be pissed about not knowing his criminal name while others did. "Why Apex?"

I answered. "Apex predator. The animal above all other animals. Killer of killers."

"He was killing it, too," Blondie told the room. "He could take down any system, defeat any hacker or security firm that challenged him. Bad MFer."

I watched Shocker and Bobby closely. They weren't surprised by this revelation. They know of Ace's skill, obviously. But he didn't tell them everything. I looked hard at the girl-beast, at the geek, more of the puzzle falling into place. "You quit when you met her," I told Ace, no question. He looked embarrassed. I grinned, *I'm right, aren't I?*

He said, "Yeah. I quit. She saved my life. I was turning into a super villain."

"What's wrong with being a super villain?" I said. The girls cut their eyes to show the worth of my wit, and I gave them double middle fingers. "Super villainous," I said with an evil grin.

Blondie shook her head at Shocker. *Men,* she shrugged. Shocker sniffed with disdain. Bobby gave everyone a bright, You-White-Folks-Are-Crazy grin while Ace continued to stress out and miss the humor. He said to my girl, "You are the first person to connect me to Apex. Many have tried."

Blondie counted off on her fingers. "You are known as the badass hacker that got arrested while working for WikiLeaks. You are a materials wizard. And, you just admitted to being Apex. I was really just fishing. For all I knew 'Wrecker' was some new program."

Shocker gave him a reprimanding scowl. *Dumbass!*

"Lovely. So what's a Wrecker?" I asked again.

"A computer. I built it to, uh..."

"Be super villain sexy?" I suggested. I held my hands up. "Hey. I get it."

He finally smiled without looking lame. "Sure. I thought we could use it. Bobby and I brought it here. It's in my car. We can set it up at your garage."

"Doable. Whacha think, Lean Meats?" I looked at Blondie.

"We'll go to the garage after we eat. Me and the super villain can test drive the Wrecker while you guys do recon with the drone." She picked up her BlackBerry from the table. "Anybody want coffee? A boutique around the corner delivers."

"She's showing off," I told the room. "She owns the place. Wait until you see how it's delivered."

"Are the delivery boys nude or something?" Shocker said. Everyone laughed. Blondie gave a cryptic smile, then sent a text to her store for the coffee orders.

I stood and walked into the kitchen. Perry had pans and utensils in use that I had forgotten I owned. He hummed jovially, the sizzle and pop of simmering oil on the stove accompanying his jam like greasy symbols and percussions. The vent over the burners sucked up the spicy, steamed smoke. I peeked into the oven's window but couldn't tell what kind of beef was making me fight drooling.

Doesn't matter, my inner wolf's slavering jaws grinned. *Meat! Meat! Meat! Meat!*

"Should be ready in a few minutes," Perry said. "I hope you like tofu."

"Toe who? Stop threatening me." My brows furrowed painfully.

Perry leaned back, laughed boomingly. "You know better than that, boy. Think I got like this eating soy imitations?" He patted his considerable girth. "You know better. Set the table. You're in my way." He pushed by me with a smile, humming once more, grabbed an oven mitt. I opened a cabinet, took out some plates.

~ ~ ~

"These," Bobby mumbled around a mouth of meat ten minutes later," are the best ribs I've ever tasted."

Perry jutted his wide jaw happily, passed a bottle of A-1 to Ace. The table was barely adequate to hold everything, its top not visible from all the food, plates and elbows. Blondie and I shared one side, facing the geek and girl-beast. Big Swoll and Perry on the ends. A pan of ribs in the center held everyone's attention. The roasted juicy meat had little cartoon wisps of scent curling enticing fingers under our noses, driving our hunger into high gear. Fried mushrooms, onions and bell peppers were sautéed in a pan next to it. A large bowl of squash and tomatoes, bowls of sweet corn and salad. French bread, toasted with thick butter and garlic.

I ate a disgusting amount. We all did.

"Oh my God," Blondie complained. "I'll need lipo' after this." She leaned back, rubbing her stomach.

"You guys want to hit the gym later?" Bobby asked, steadily forking it in.

"We'll do it," I said, resisting the urge to grab a fifth rib. I sighed, pushed my chair back. Glanced at Perry, whose eyes were enlivened by the meal and its effects on us. *Damn you. I'll have to double up my cardio in the morning to burn off all this good shit.* I grimaced at him, reached for another rib. Perry barked a laugh.

A loud, high-pitched beeping sounded from outside the front door. Blondie stood quickly, flashing perfect teeth. "That's the coffee." We stood and followed, their faces curious about the delivery service that beeps rather than knocks.

The beeping continued. As we neared the door we could hear the sound of buffeted wind, as if a huge fan were on HIGH. Blondie opened the door like one of those *The Price Is Right* models and a small four-rotor helicopter hovered in our faces, its electric motors spinning incredibly fast, though silent, the roaring wind resistance its only exhaust. It was a Draganfly X4-P, a very light, very strong, all carbon fiber aircraft with a camera and insulated box hanging between its skids.

"Hi Crystal," Blondie told the camera, carefully opening the box. Removed two medium coffees. Handed them to Shocker, Ace. Closed the box.

"Hi ma'am," chirped a female voice from a small

speaker not visible. The Draganfly backed away and another one hovered in its place. Crystal continued talking on this one. "Four coffees, ma'am. Is there anything else you need?"

Blondie took the coffee from Draganfly #2. "No. I'll text you if I do. Thanks."

"Okay," she chirped, sounding exactly like the preppy teen she was. "Have a nice day everybody!"

The Draganflies fanned away quickly, the rotor thrust fading then vanishing. Everyone stared in the direction they went. Their open mouths and intrigued eyes made my girl very pleased. Ace was still waving slightly, unconsciously, tongue poking out the side of his confounded mouth. He realized he was still waving bye to Crystal, stopped, looked down at his coffee, a 12 oz. mocha latte that added a kid-like smile to his lame geek features. He sipped it.

Blondie *thrummed* from his reaction to the whole thing. Shocker stared at her with a bursting *What the fuck???* load of questions pushing out her hazel eyes, veins wriggling freaky-deaky on her over-developed upper body.

Bobby slurped his coffee. "Ah..." He elbowed his new pal. "All right. Spill it, princess. We need to know how you've transported us into the future."

Blondie elbowed him back, closed the door and touched her espresso to his. Sipped it. "Mmm. It's good, huh? The boutique's name is *Blondie's*. We deliver coffee, pastries, flowers, and toiletries - anything under two pounds - to the local community."

"Two pound payload?" Shocker inquired. "That's why you needed two helicopters to deliver four coffees?"

"Yep."

"Did you build them?"

Blondie shook her head. "Draganfly Innovations manufactures them. I saw them on the 'Net a couple years ago and wondered why no one was using them for consumer delivery. I had just opened Blondie's and thought I'd test them in my business model."

"It's perfect," Shocker nodded. "No delivery expenses other than the pennies it costs to charge batteries." She sipped thoughtfully. Everyone sat down in the living room. Perry grinned and walked back to the kitchen to begin cleaning.

Blondie set her coffee on a table, gestured with her hands. "The Draganfly X-four-p is thirty-four inches wide, twelve inches tall. The motors are brushless, very quiet. The four booms holding the motors and the camera body are carbon fiber."

"Tech?" the geek wanted to know.

"Flight time?" Shocker asked.

My girl gave her I Love Being the Center of Attention smile, said, "A powerful on-board processor with eleven sensors make it stable and easy to fly. The camera is vibration-isolated from both the chassis and camera mount. The entire rig weighs four and a half pounds, and can fly for thirty minutes on one charge."

Shocker's eyes rolled up in calculation. She said, "I'm guessing it could make deliveries five miles away and still have enough juice to get home."

"Yeah, about that. The twelve-megapixel camera takes incredible images. You can program it to go to a location, snap photos or vids, and return on autopilot. Employees at Blondie's take orders by phone or Web and load the purchases on the Draganflies. Type the address into a laptop and they will fly there by themselves. When they reach their destination the autopilot is switched off and an employee takes the controls while talking to the customer. You've seen the payload box. A magnetic card reader is mounted on it. Customers take out their purchase and swipe their card."

"What about vandalism?" Bobby inquired, standing in

front of the TV.

Blondie shrugged. "Hasn't been an issue yet. But if some dumbass kids ever try to take one down they're in for a surprise."

"Such as???" Shocker prompted, no fan of suspense.

Her face turned sneaky. She mimed spraying a can. "A squirt of pepper spray. There's a small canister on-board with a tiny solenoid to discharge it. The evasive software should take it out of danger before that happens though; sonar sensors warn it of any approaching objects. The payload box also opens from underneath. It could drop two cups of scalding coffee on someone." She tittered at the thought.

Shocker smiled wickedly. "That could be very useful."

"I know, right?"

As Blondie continued to expound on her concept, I watched the girls, amazed that they had seemed to put aside their differences. It was a gradual change, built on grudging respect. I was forced to revise my assessment that they would never be friends even if they were paid to. "Hungh," I said.

"What?" Ace asked me.

I jerked my head up at the chattering women. Bobby grinned knowingly at me, at his inquisitive friend. I said, "They're no longer keeping score."

"That we can tell," Bobby added in a low rumble.

"Oh," Ace said.

The girls abruptly quieted, eyeing us suspiciously. Bobby suddenly found his espresso very interesting. Ace turned a guilty color. I gave my #1 Mr. Good Guy smile. "Nice to see you vixens aren't trying to compare boobies anymore."

Shocker looked at Blondie, annoyed. "Is he always asking for it?"

For an answer, my blonde lynx lunged at me with a jab,

her little fist thudding into my shoulder. I nearly flipped the chair over backwards trying to avoid it. Everyone laughed, the girls flanking me as I stood to fend off the play.

"All right now," I warned. Duck, catch, block. Pivot. Moved around the couch. I bared my teeth, held my hands up. "You were warned. Now you've awakened an ancient evil, *The Super Spank Monsters*." My horror movie murderer voice had Bobby wheezing in humor.

"Oh shit!" Blondie squeaked as I jumped the divan, spun her around and pelted her cakes with several hard slaps. "Ow!" She rubbed her curves in pain, jumping up and down on her toes, face anguished.

Shocker came at me with a grin that turned ugly as I blocked her blow, spun her around, and *Whop!* Nailed her buttocks as hard as I could. "Son of a *mmm*," she bit her lip, holding the offended area with both hands.

"Super Spank Monsters score!" I crowed, fists over my head, feet shuffling a victory dance.

Ace looked at me like he wanted to say something about me spanking his wife. Bobby murmured something next to his ear and he nodded. *OK. This isn't flirting*, his eyes revealed.

The girls turned on me with coiled fists and vengeful eyes. Still playful. But a more *intent* playful. The feeling of uncertainty no man likes when faced by an evil-eyed woman? It grabbed my nuts and twisted away a substantial amount of my confidence.

Blondie has serious help, my subconscious told the Super Spank Monsters. *You're in trou-blle ...*

Jump back over the couch. Block Shocker, slip Blondie. Ow! Ow! Eat two gut punches, one in the kidney. Block, catch, push them away. It became too much, their four fists able to get by my defense as they chased me around the living room. I slipped behind Big Swoll, pushed him into my attackers. They giggled, threatened to hit him. He held his hands up, wanting no part of their drama, and I tripped on the *fucking* table, sprawling on my stomach, grunting as they jumped on top of me. Breath whooshing at the intense right-hand that landed below my ribs. They giggled like mad women, bombarding me with frogging knuckles. I covered face, stomach, face again...

"Ugh! Oof! Ow! Crap, dammit, quit, *okay!* You win. YIELD DAMMIT!"

"When you kids are done tickling each other," Perry said, standing over us wiping his hands on a towel. "Maybe you can tell me why all those Vietnamese gangsters just pulled up out front."

~ ~ ~

"They know it was you," Big Guns told me and Blondie. Glanced at Shocker. "I put my boys around the building in case Diep sends his riders here."

"Here for what?" Shocker said standing. "To get their butts handed to them again? We'll handle them."

Big Guns grinned chrome. The memory of her ferocious assault on the 211 earlier came out in an amused grunt. "I'm sure you will. But I doubt they'll want to get close enough for that again. They'll try to knock you off in a drive-by."

I grimaced. *The apartment is no longer safe. We'll have to move.* I knew this was a possible consequence, so I prepared for it. Just didn't want to do it so early in the game. "Fuck. Any idea how they tracked us?"

He nodded. "Vietech."

Blondie's eyes widened with alarm. "That's not good."

"Who's Vietech?" Ace asked, standing next to his girl. Perry walked out of the kitchen, folded his arms and listened.

Blondie looked at Ace. "Hacker for the Tiger Society. He's based in New Orleans. M.I.T. grad, masters in computer science. He has a rep for designing topnotch spyware."

Ace gave a cocky half smile, one eye squinted. He wasn't impressed. "Never heard of him. Of course, I've been out of play for a while." He talked like major criminal hacking was a video game. I liked him better by the minute. "An amateur could have tracked us here. There are cameras all over this area. He could have found your faces and then ran them through various databases for identification. Should we run a campaign to keep him busy?" His fingers typed the air, eager to engage in cyber warfare.

Blondie's lips smirked. "Let's do it." She spun around to look up at me, put a hand on my chest. My Johnson noted a tingling warmth spreading from her touch. "We're going to the garage to see if we can locate Vietech and shut him down. You need me for anything?"

I shook my head. "I'll call you."

She kissed me and hugged Perry. Ace followed her out the front door after hugging the girl-beast.

Big Guns looked at me, jerked his head at the door. "You want me to put an escort on them? I can have Gat and Vu follow."

"Nah. No offense big guy, but I don't want your guys knowing where the garage is. Not yet." I crossed my arms. "Just like you have informers in the Tiger Society, they surely have rats in the Dragon Family."

Big Guns nodded. "True. It's a raw business."

"I thought we were going to do recon or something," Bobby said from the couch. "Yeah. I don't feel right just sitting here. This place has been compromised," Shocker added, sitting down next to Big Swoll.

"We will. First though, let's consider our next mode of attack," I suggested. Big Guns looked out the window behind the TV, making sure his crew were alert. He turned and sat in the chair. I looked around at everyone. "The Tiger Society has a racket on dozens of businesses in Biloxi and D'Iberville. The Two-Eleven and OBG collect 'protection fees' every Friday. I think we should disrupt their pick-up."

Big Guns' eyes had darkened. He said, "They have no honor. They take and give nothing back."

Shocker blew out a breath, arms folded tightly under her boobies. "Does the Dragon Family have extortion rackets like that?"

Big Guns glared at her. A vein pulsed in his forehead. Voice choking back anger he said, "The Dragon Family used to provide real protection to the people the Tiger Society are ripping off and assaulting. They gave freely, knowing we used some of the money to benefit our people. We never threatened or beat them."

The girl-beast looked abashed. "Oh," she said, eyes downcast. Bobby chuckled, gave her a *cheer up* elbow.

I put a hand on Big Guns' shoulder. "An honorable gangster. The last of the breed." He turned his pulsing vein on me. I ignored it. "The Tiger Society's grunts do the pick-ups, when? Today is Friday."

"Around five in the 'Ville. Then they hit a few places on Division Street and Popps Ferry Road."

I glanced at my watch. 4:40 pm. "Timely," I told them as if I hadn't planned this yesterday. "It's a ten minute drive to the spot I want to hit them."

"What's the plan?" Shocker quizzed. She and Bobby stood, ready to take care of business. Talk of people being extorted had put that fire back in her eyes.

"We wait until they collect from everyone, then jump them. We'll spank them for their transgressions and return the money to the victims."

"All Robin Hood, and shit," Bobby said grinning. His chest flexed, muscles jumping up impressively. Big Guns looked like he wanted to flex in challenge. Bobby gave the Viet gangster an expression that invited, *Any time little man.*

"Nice plan, Mister President." Shocker bumped

knuckles with me.

I grinned at her. My canines felt especially sharp. "President says, L*et's ride.*"

Everyone thanked Perry for the meal. He reiterated his offer for first-aid. "I know you guys will need it," he said walking out the door. Shocker rubbed her scarred shoulders. I rubbed my forearm, a memento from a scrap with three drunks. Broken liquor bottles kinda hurt. We tried not to mug Perry's back as he climbed into his truck. The 454 big block propelled the '49 GMC away with lovely bellowing waves of turbo-muffled sound.

I locked the apartment after everyone stepped out, punched a few buttons on my phone to set the alarm. If anyone shows up here motion sensor activated cameras will instantly send a video of the intruder to my BlackBerry. The four of us walked out to greet Big Guns' crew, six members of the Royal Family, a subset of the Dragon Family. Their leader told them to stand down. They followed orders like pros and three tricked Hondas *brrapted* away seconds later. We got into the lime Prelude.

Big Guns took his time driving us to D'Iberville. The sun was still blazing hot, the breeze entering the open windows just barely enough to keep us from sweating. The rooftops of the one-and-two-story buildings we passed were distorted by simmering air. Downtown D'Iberville was booming, cars sloshing around parking lots like bacteria on a petri dish, packing into rush hour traffic, people getting off work and hurrying to their establishment of preference.

Big Guns pointed to a row of businesses to our left, a long plaza with coffee and print shops, several oriental restaurants and clothing outlets. He said, "Vietnamese own most of those. We used to collect donations from them. But that changed. They claim they can't afford donations now, and hang their heads in shame at the lie. They give it to the Tiger Society now." He gripped the steering wheel audibly, golden brown hands paling.

I watched the buildings from the passenger seat, scheming. Shocker reached around the driver's seat and squeezed Big Guns' arm, hard. In a voice laced with we're-about-to-kick-some-ass she said, "We'll just have to change it back."

He looked at her in the rear view mirror, showing silver determination. *Damn right*, he grunted, feeling her energy. The girl-beast had that effect on me, too. She vibrated raw, freaky-quick power. For whatever reason, she made me want to do better. In everything. Once again I felt a blanket of euphoria from getting to work with her.

"Let's park over there," I said pointing to a small grassy area behind a gas station. "We can get out and get loose."

Big Guns grunted acknowledgment, turned left without a blinker, and we darted through an intersection, low-rider buzzing a 400hp turbo-charged four banger that vibrated our bodies in a very gratifying fashion. We passed BP pumps, the station's windowed front, and turned into the parking spot nearest the rear of the white brick building. We opened the gull wing doors and climbed out, ignoring the teenagers that ogled us and the car.

I surveyed the area to make sure we could observe without being observed. The gas station was at the end of the plaza, right on the corner of an intersection. The grass behind it was landscaped by concrete curbs, a triangle of lawn with a propane tank and air-compressor in a cage for customers' use. The Prelude was out of sight. We walked around the corner, stood on the grass and studied the coffee shop at the far end of the plaza. I said, "The caffeine dealers get hit first. We wait until they collect from everyone then hit them. Okay?" I looked at Shocker. "They will rough up the owners on general principle. You have to let it happen."

"I'll try," she said, then sighed skeptically. I had a feeling someone was going to have to grab her to keep her from interfering.

Not going to be me ...

Bobby gripped one of his fists. "So they smack 'em around? Why don't we take 'em out before they start collecting?"

"We have to win over the people," I said. "With contrast. Joy is best felt after strife." I looked at my Viet friend.

He grunted agreement. "It will be a lesson for everyone. We will be stronger afterwards. It is our way."

The waiting sucked. Finally, a gold Acura turned into the plaza and pulled up in front of the coffee shop, blocking several cars from leaving. Three guys got out, Vietnamese gangsters in nice clothes and jewelry, stylish hair, one in a ball cap. Hardcore scowls narrowing their criminal eyes. They gestured and taunted the patrons attempting to leave.

"The driver stayed in the car. It looks like they are going to rob the place," Shocker said, teeth bared. I could sense a change beginning to overtake her.

"They are," I said, "And we are going to rob the robbers."

She gave me an impatient glance. "I don't like this."

"We wait."

My imperative tone made her eyes narrow at me, *I don't like* that *either*.

The trio of thugs came out of the shop a few minutes later, one of them looking around, the other two holding large cups and pastry boxes they had helped themselves to, laughing, shouting back through the open door in Vietnamese. They got into the car. The Acura's rear tires barked, they drove a short distance to a small restaurant that specialized in oriental food.

"We should stop this," Bobby rumbled. Shocker raised her eyebrows at me. When Big Guns grunted exasperation Big Swoll said, "What? I like to eat there." He shook his huge head. "This isn't right." He turned to watch our targets.

The gangsters got back out of the Acura and swaggered into the restaurant. One of them slapped down what looked like a barbequed duck hanging in the picture window. Several patrons could be seen hurriedly getting up from their tables, paying and leaving. The extortionists' loud laughter was cut off as the door closed. The driver bobbed his head, fingers tapping on the steering wheel, the front of the car facing us, sixty yards away.

Too much time went by. I couldn't see them but knew something bad was happening inside the restaurant. The driver sensed it too, his enthusiastic jamming on pause as he stared anxiously through the duck-less window. Sometimes marks resisted, or the thugs would be overzealous intimidating them. Either way it was unwanted trouble for everyone involved.

"Just wait," I reminded myself.

The door burst open suddenly, some kind of beaded decoration scattering on the sidewalk, broken. A small Asian man in a white apron was shoved outside violently. The three thugs crowded him, walking out, one holding brown paper bags in each arm. The restaurant owner was pleading with them, voice high, rapid. The larger of the thugs slapped him and I had to grab Shocker's arms to hold her back. It felt like grabbing a bag of pythons; she writhed and seethed, on the verge of eruption, dueling for control of her inner fight junkie, shoulders pulsating under my grip.

The driver waved at his comrades impatiently, constantly checking the mirrors for the D'Iberville PD. The three idiots laughed at the antagonized man, who begged them not to take whatever was in the bags. The biggest of our marks punched the poor guy in his stomach, knocking him to the cement, arms hugging his apron pitifully. An older lady came trotting out the door shrieking in Vietnamese, throwing rolls of bread at the goons tormenting her husband. Biggest Idiot turned and punched her full in the face. She yelped into silence, falling out of sight, inside.

"*Fuck that,*" the girl-beast snarled at me and them both. She snatched my hands off her and exploded, sprinting in their direction, brass knuckles appearing on her fists.

Bobby thundered an excited, "Let's get 'em!"

Big Guns grunted, turned to prepare the car for a speedy exit.

I twirled a finger at Big Swoll. "Let's hurry," I said, lunging into a run.

I had no idea Shocker could run so goddamn fast. I shouldn't have been surprised, though. She crossed the intersection like Super Frogger, and raced down the sidewalk in front of the businesses faster than belief, legs blurring.

The driver saw her first. He had no time to shout a warning before she was on them. Biggest Idiot caught the worst of it. She hit him with a right-hand that had all her weight and speed behind it. The brass smack and wail of pain was heard by everyone in the plaza. Shoppers gawked as his arms flew out straight, face distorted in surprised hurt, his butt thumping on an iron drainage cover hard enough to boom like a huge brass drum. That was it for him; he was out of the game, destined for the emergency room. He lay on his back, exhaling to sleep.

Shocker pivoted-flowed-zeroing in on her next targets. I don't know what made their faces freak out the most: that they were being attacked or that it was a girl doing it. They were lost for time. Shocker closed on them with whistling uppercuts and hooks, her feet and fists in time, shoulders and hips rolling like hydraulic mechanisms. Their arms came up to try and block her assault but were simply too slow and untrained. Her metallic punches found wide open bull's-eyes. They went backwards then down, faces split and leaking, one of them knocked into a semi-conscious state by a hook on the chin, neck twisting suddenly, sharply.

Our boots pounded to a stop in front of the Acura. I put my hands on my waist and complained, "Dammit. You didn't leave anything for *us*." The driver gaped at me, at the humongous black dude towering in front of his car. At his friends laid out on the sidewalk. He looked back at the girl-beast, too terrified to make a decision.

The legendary fighter turned inhuman eyes on me. "Fuck that," she growled. She turned her attention back to her targets, fists coiled. *Is that foam at the corner of her mouth?* Her breaths were slow and measured, her focus scary intense. The mark started scrambling backwards, climbing over the man in the apron, desperately trying to put distance between himself and the predator.

"Oh no you don't," Bobby told the driver. He grabbed the frightened gangster through the open driver's window and snatched him out of the car, forehead banging hard on the door pillar. The guy's babbling queries turned into a full-throated scream as Big Swoll spun and threw his catch into the restaurant's picture window. It was so incredibly funny because Bobby outweighed the guy by 150 pounds, his enormous upper body effortlessly tossing the thug like a sack of expired dog food. The screaming continued through the exploding glass, silencing as he crashed into whatever broke inside the restaurant. The woman revived at this additional chaos, standing shakily, her shrieking once again echoing out across the plaza.

"Oops," Bobby said, wincing. "My bad." I laughed in delight as his big ass walked up on the sidewalk, helped the aproned man to his feet. Dusted off his back for him. "Sorry about your window."

The man looked around wildly, nodding, shook up badly. Still gripping his stomach, he shuffled inside and put an arm around his wife, who kept making very annoying sounds of terror. They stared at us like we weren't real. *What planet did you monsters come from?* their rounded eyes and trembling lips emoted.

"It's too late for that," Bobby told the guy crabbing away from Shocker. The thug grabbed weakly at the front of his waist, pulled up his shirt. The girl-beast calmly stalked him, allowing him to think about what was coming. Her fists clenched in veined glory. Eyes insanely alight. She put a pink Nike Shox on his hand groping for the gun. Pushed down harshly. He garbled something that signified pain.

Seeing the Shocker was in no shape to give a speech, I stepped up next to her. Pointed and laughed at her victim. "You look fucked up," I observed. He garbled, eyes agonized. She pushed down harder, crushing more than his hand.

Ow, my Johnson flinched.

His fingers widened. She let up and his hands shot out to the sides of his head in surrender. I tisked him. "It isn't your day, pal. Your boss put you in a high-risk job position. You should complain."

"I hope you have health insurance," Bobby said, dragging the guy he had thrown through the window out onto the sidewalk.

"Who? Why..." Gargle, cough. He rubbed his throat, and I realized he must have caught a punch there.

I held up a finger. "Shut up. I'll do the talking. You'll listen, or the girl-beast will open your ears for you. Got it?" The Shocker's eyes and nostrils flared at me, *Girl-beast??? Fuck that!* I ignored her.

The other gangster gave up crawling away, slumped over in front of a clothing shop, breathing raggedly. I smiled in his direction, very pleased. Looked back at the idiot in front of us. "I want you to pass on a message..."

VII. A Little Late

"So I asked him how many girls he was fucking. I was like, you wanna be with me? The other girls have to go," Blondie told Shocker.

"You could have said all this without me being here, you know," I pointed out. And was ignored.

Shocker grilled her for more gossip. "What did he say? How many?" She glanced at me, a hint of disapproval wrinkling her nose.

Blondie smiled slyly, looked at me. "He dropped his head like a chump and muttered," she deepened her voice to imitate me, "'Two.'"

"Hey, I don't mutter like that." Again, I was ignored. Bobby and Ace, flanking me on the small couch, were nearly out of breath from laughing. *Why is that so funny? I asked her out and she set rules.* "Ha! Ha! Fuck both of you."

The bastards laughed even harder.

Shocker gave a "Ha!" that said she knew I was full of crap. "You didn't believe him, of course."

"Hell no," my girl said, sly quirk still on her lips. "There were four or five girls at the gym pretending to work out while competing for his attention. I knew he was fucking them as soon as I walked in the door. *Two???* Right. I just stared at him and he finally said, 'Three.' I kept staring, gave him the Yeah Right look." She demonstrated, bent hand on waist, eyebrows curved in skepticism. "He needed to be honest if he wanted me and he knew it. He got all flustered and shit. Then he growled at me, 'All right! Six, okay?'"

She laughed, flipped hair off her shoulders.

"*Six?*" Shocker looked at me in disgust. "You pig."

"That's Mister President Pig to you, girl-beast freak."

She shook her head, looked at Blondie. "You guys met in a gym?" She leaned back in the chair behind the desk. A breeze came in through the shed door, billowing strands of dark hair over her hazel eyes.

"Yep. I had just got out of jail." Blondie walked around the drone, heels clicking, composing the story of how we met. I tried to suffer it in silence. "I went to this gym to work off some stress and saw a ripped guy fist dancing on a heavy bag. He looked like bad news, but I thought I could impose my will and maybe turn him into something." She pushed one shoulder up, smiling behind it, and chortled a sharp feminine sound that made my skin heat up. "Plus, I wanted him to teach me boxing."

"Again. I'm *right here*. I thought girls were supposed to gossip about their men when they weren't present." I pointed at them. "Observe proper etiquette."

I got a "Pfff" from the girl-beast.

Shocker watched Blondie in suspense. Bobby and Ace tried to pretend they weren't here, though their poorly restrained snickers sort of messed that up. I felt like everyone was riding down on me, and wanted to be somewhere else very badly. Shocker asked, "So he stopped being a whore to be with you?" Blondie nodded in satisfaction. Shocker eyed me, still suspicious, protective of her new friend.

Oh, that's just wonderful, my subconscious sighed.

"Why were you in jail?" she asked Blondie.

My girl gave a brilliant flash of teeth that I couldn't help but return, skin tingling inside the warmth. We were finally done talking about me. I hope. She said, "I had to promote a book."

"A book," Shocker said slowly. She looked at me. "Sex book?"

I shook my head. "Nope. A novel about a little girl that

is murdered by someone in her family. It's good. I read it twice."

"A murder mystery," Blondie confirmed.

"You're a *writer?* " Shocker's skepticism was palpable.

She shrugged. "I wanted to go to school for it, but my parents wouldn't support me. I wrote *Leslie's Diary* during my senior year of high school. I couldn't get any help publishing it, so I self-published on the Internet. I didn't know shit about marketing novels and couldn't sell very many. But I knew how to market myself." She unconsciously stepped into a sexy pose. My tongue decided to wet my lips for some reason. She continued. "I needed to get the media's attention, however I could. So I caught an assault charge and went to jail."

"Assault?" Ace inquired. "What did you do?"

She smiled at the fond memory. "I kicked a cop in the face, then sprayed him with his own pepper spray."

"My hero," Bobby rumbled. Shocker and Ace grinned excited agreement. I felt amazed by their enthusiasm over an officer being assaulted.

Blondie soaked it up, the sexy badass, nearly preening. "The papers printed all kinds of crap, like 'Daughter of Prominent Lawyers in Jail for Assaulting Policeman.'" She gave an exulted squeal.

"You have parents?" I said. Then, "You have parents that are lawyers???" *No wonder she shares my dislike of attorneys...*

She pretended I hadn't said that. Everyone else glanced at me like I was a complete duffer.

Blondie said, "I knew my parents wouldn't bond me out after the fight we had. Go to fucking law school? Right. So I did three months in the county, no biggie, a first-time offender." She pursed her lips, then said, "I had a plan for their ass. I had my girl open a dozen e-mail accounts and contact news reporters. She masqueraded as all sorts of people - Bible thumpers, busy-bodies, housewives, et cetera. These 'concerned citizens' wanted to know how violent, potential cop killers were selling books while in jail. They were outraged by the thought of prisoners making money while God-fearing free people had trouble finding jobs. There had just been a story about prisoners with cell phones being on MySpace, so prisoners were a current issue.

"The jail guards shook me down nearly every day after that. They were pissed about reporters showing up demanding to know how I got a phone, and how I was running a business while I should be being punished for assaulting a law enforcement officer." She laughed, hand pressed between her boobies. "I found out that a dozen God-fearing citizens, even fictitious ones, can cause a hellacious response from law enforcement, and the media."

"I thought you didn't sell any books?" Shocker said.

Blondie gave a devious smile. "I wasn't. But they didn't know that. All those thousands of people that saw the story on TV or in the papers didn't know that. All of a sudden hundreds of copies of *Leslie's Diary* started selling. My parents' name drew a lot of attention, and people in general wanted to see what all the fuss was about. By the time they let me out, I had made over sixty thousand dollars."

"Whoa," Ace said.

"Nice," Bobby agreed.

"Hmm." Shocker's brows furrowed. She was having trouble accepting Blondie's work as something cool. She maintained an on-the-fence expression and said, "Relatively cheap way to market a book. What did your parents say?"

"Don't know. We haven't spoken in eleven years."

"Hey," I wanted to know. "When did you get parents?"

She rolled her eyes. Looked at Shocker. "Anyway. That's how I met Meat-head and got into crime."

Shocker's features waned, her voice low, retrieving from memory. "You reminded me of something Coach used to tell me, a lesson he gave to all the pros he worked with." She cleared her throat and strengthened her voice. "'It doesn't matter if they buy a ticket to see you win, or buy a ticket to see you lose. *As long as they buy a ticket*.'" She let out a heavy breath.

Blondie tried smiling, but faltered, remembering that was her coach, too, and he was no longer around to impart such wisdom. "Yeah. That sounds like Eddy. That's basically what I did to promote the book. Bad publicity is still publicity."

"How did you get into crime, Razor?" Bobby asked me, steering the conversation away from tears.

"I learned how to work on cars from the bikers who raised me. I stole them. Sold them."

"Sold them?" Ace prompted.

"Sometimes I would switch VIN plates and just sell the stolen vehicles. Then I figured out a better scam. I would place ads on the Internet claiming I had high-end cars - BMW's, Mercedes, cars of that class. I posted random pictures I found in *Motor Trend* to make the ads look legit. People would call me and negotiate. It took a week or two sometimes, but eventually someone would offer cash to get a better deal. I'd meet them somewhere and take it."

"So you never actually had the cars?" Ace asked.

"Didn't need them."

"Whoa," he breathed.

Shocker's head shook in disapproval throughout my story. She told me, "Shame. All that talent, and it was wasted on scams."

I mugged her. "Okay, Miss Goody Pooh Shoes. I'm not ragging you for escaping prison and being a regular on *America's Most Wanted*. Don't stick your prissy nose too far in the air."

She still shook her head, but smiled. Laughed.

"*Excusez-moi,* Mister President."

"Dear," Ace said to his girl. "Did the big ebony tank really throw someone through a window?"

She looked at him and nodded, on the verge of a huge giggle. "And I thought I was mad at those guys. Bobby jerked that idiot out of the car and tossed him like a dirty diaper."

"It was an accident," Bobby said defensively. "I told the man I'd pay for his window."

"He'll really pay for it, huh?" I said to Shocker. She nodded with a proud twist of her lips.

I turned to Bobby. "I wouldn't sweat it, big guy. That dude was happy to get his daughter's birthday present back. He's good."

Shocker frowned up. "I can't believe those assholes took a bunch of costume jewelry."

"Was it valuable?" Ace asked.

"To them it was," I said. "To their eight-year-old daughter it was priceless. Those gangsters likely took it just to be cruel. They would have thrown it away."

"Fuckers," Blondie said with feeling. "Got what they deserved." She lapsed into silence, looking a little hurt from missing all the fun. She pointed her delicate chin at me. "Where's the video, Raz? I want to see it."

"Big Guns recorded some of it from the car. It's on his phone."

She nodded, *Thank you,* and grabbed her phone off the desk to send a message to her Viet friend.

I looked out the door. The streetlights far below us had been flooding the ground with eerie orange hues for over an hour. The din of heavy Friday night traffic echoed around the garage, condos behind us, out into the open, dark blue and purple sky, cloudy and moonless over the Gulf. A premonition absorbed my thoughts as I inhaled the cooling air, one of caution. I stood and walked outside. Looked around, knowing I wouldn't see anything but the roof of the garage, our vehicles, the open air beyond its edges. *Am I forgetting something?*

I decided to take a quick peek at the surveillance monitors, walking over to the other shed, the lab. I reached for the door handle and the *fucking* power went out. The sudden blackness inside the drone shed hushed my squad.

"Forget to pay your bill, Mister President?" Shocker said, walking up next to me. Everyone followed her, Blondie looking startled, them smiling.

Their humor vanished when they saw my face. "They're here," I told them, tense, muscles priming for action.

"How do you know?" Shocker said, also fully alert.

"Because they disabled the generator." I turned and jogged the twenty feet to the roof entrance. "You know you should have installed a generator up here, you stupid MFer," I derided myself. *And you should have been monitoring the cameras too...*

I skidded to a stop in front of the entrance right as the thick steel door unlocked and began sliding open. My mind raced. *How did they unlock it? Remote power source attached to the keypad circuit. They have a pro that hacked the code ... Do they have guns? Of course they do, dumbass! They know goddamn well they can't beat you with their hands!*

I had no time to think of a defense, or even to make a run for the rapell rope we keep tied near the edge of the roof (which was a Capt. Jack Sparrow move I would never do). My only chance was to try and bullshit my way out of immediate death. *How did they find us?* I couldn't blame anyone but myself. I knew the consequences of working with a team. That's why I've never done it before.

The door clunked to a stop, fully open. "Hi pal," I told Diep's scowling mug and the half dozen gunmen in front of him, semi-auto pistols twinkling death in their tense hands.

Diep didn't respond to my greeting. They pushed through the entrance. I stepped backwards, palms facing them. The gangsters spread out around me, three of them drawing down on my crew. The other three backed up Diep, their incensed leader that stared at me with a murderous hunger. I eyed the gun barrels warily. Looked at the Elder Tiger. His right arm was in a cast up to the elbow, dark blue fiberglass. Bruises stood out around his sunglasses, chin beard making his mouth remarkably merciless. His glasses flashed a glance at my crew's angry looks. He said to me, "Razor. The notorious con artist and boxing champion."

"Retired and retired," I said amiably.

"So you quit the confidence game to get into extortion rackets? Seems odd. I got your message. You had me convinced you were really a new rival gang. Until my investigation turned up the truth." He motioned to one of his subordinates, a muscle-bound gangster in a blue warm-up suit. He looked at his boss with round eyes in a mixed, freckled face. Diep told him in a disappointed tone, "*Phong. Anh em cua may bi mat mac. May phai lay mac cha lai.*"

My brain heard, "Phong. Your brothers have lost face. You have to face nose and face."

Phong, the leader of the 211, stepped forward and swung his gun at my head. It was quick, but I saw it coming through Fight mode eyes and shifted back, his arm brushing mine. I checked myself from counter punching and just pushed him away. Phong swung again, faster, missing without me even moving, anger reddening his face, neck, arms.

I gave Diep a reproachful look. "What? You think I'm just going to stand here and let him hit me?"

"You're right, of course. What was I thinking?" Diep looked at Phong. "Shoot him in the leg."

"No you're NOT!" Blondie shouted, storming past the gangsters pointing guns at her. They yelled in their foreign tongue, grabbed her, and I waved to her it was okay before she attacked them or they shot her.

I looked at Phong, who uncannily resembled Bolo Yeung from my favorite martial arts movies. My legs squirmed uneasily. He smiled at me, raised the gun. Took careful aim and must have thought I'd just stand there and let him plug me. *What's up with that?*

He squeezed the trigger as I darted to the side. The bullet's sonic boom was swallowed by the open air, the round taking a chunk out of the concrete just behind me. Phong glanced at Diep, deepened his snarl and squeezed off two more shots at my legs. The years of boxing drills enabled my legs to move and change directions very explosively. But not so fast as to avoid a 9 mm slug moving 1200 feet per second.

The first one missed, ricocheting off the concrete, making the gangsters around Blondie flinch as she screeched over the bullet's whine through the air. The second shot hit me in the left shin, barely missing the bone. It burned a hole through my leg and exited at the side of my calf, sending a message to my brain to demand that I jump up and down and scream in pain. I obliged, hopping on one foot, gasping loud curses, and Phong stepped forward with an inspired swing of his weapon, the hot barrel slamming into my cheekbone, sizzling my lip. I went down.

"Rarrr," I sucked in through clenched teeth. I tried to control my breathing, gripping my leg above the wound, as if that would make it stop hurting. On the plus side, it felt so bad I didn't even feel my swelling face.

"Now. That's better," Diep said, as if training a dog to sit on command.

"You piece of shit," Shocker told the Viet overlord. Through my trembling vision I noticed the girl-beast was so hyped up she was glowing like some kind of steroidal angel. I expected to see wings sprout from her muscled back and fold down in anger. Ace watched her and the guns pointed at her, terrified, hand gripping her wrist tightly.

Focus on the problem in your hands, my leg throbbed. I glanced at my girl to make sure she was okay. She watched me so intently, ready to go wide-open-lunatic at any indication from me. Bobby stood behind her, head and shoulders taller, huge hands gripping her arms, more for consolation than restraint.

"Keep an eye out for their friend the sniper," Diep told his men. He looked closely at Bobby, Ace. "Was it one of you?" He held up his cast, rubbed it with his good hand, nails perfectly manicured, gold watch gleaming wealth. "For some reason I doubt it."

He looked around the roof slowly, shifted his attention to a methodical sweep of the condo building behind the garage. He pulled out his phone. Dialed and spoke to someone in Vietnamese. It was too quick to catch much of it, but I got the gist. He ordered more men to check the condo building. *How many of them are down there?*

I cursed my luck again. I wonder what, exactly, had led them to us. When it was just me and Blondie on a job I could see all the possibilities almost immediately. With more people comes more unknown variables.

Problems. Just say problems, the prick between my ears scorned.

Blood had filled my boot, disturbingly warm and syrupy. The wound was wet and weirdly numb, yet rang with fire as if a great bell was tolling reverberations of hurt up my leg and spine, into my aching neck and lolling head. I could *feel* the tunnel that had been bored through my calf. It told me that if I tried to stand or flex my foot in any way I would seriously regret it. My neck was straining so hard speech felt impossible. In other words, it's unlikely I could fight or talk my way out of this now.

"Wonderful," I gasped.

"Isn't it?" Diep turned around to smile at me. "Revenge best served cold, and so forth."

"How did you find us?" I tried to growl. It came out a low wheeze.

His eyes nearly closed in pleasure, and I recognized the tell-tale signs of a painkiller buzz. The hospital probably gave him Demerol, the lucky bastard. He was very high. *Maybe he'll make mistakes...* He spoke in an annoying, I Bested You voice. "A photo of her," he pointed at Blondie, "standing six stories in the air, on this roof, with a stupendous sunset over the water behind her." He waved grandly in the direction of the Gulf, the sky black and well past sunset. He shook his head and talked to me like a pro addressing an amateur. "You really should be more careful what you put on the Internet. Geo tags can prove very troublesome."

I grunted in disgust. So a new team member wasn't at fault. I looked at my girl, furious. *You just had to huh? I'll deal with you later.*

She dropped her eyes, knowing she had messed up bad. She had broken our agreement, a Rule vital to our security: take no photos or videos where we dwell. Diep's people had found us by GPS coordinates logged in the details of a photo. A goddamn geo tag. An amateur error. She must have posted it on Facebook, Instagram, or some shit.

Diep waved his cast. "Tie them up. Take their phones." He pushed a speed dial button on his phone, held it to his ear and shouted in rapid-fire Vietnamese while gangsters secured our hands behind us with plastic zip-ties and searched our pockets for phones.

The prick that patted me down found my razor and unsheathed it. He turned it over in his hands for a moment, smiling at the gems, stuck it in his back pocket. I told him, "I'll be coming for that." He scowled and punched me in the stomach.

"Tie his leg, motherfucker!" Blondie demanded of Diep. "He'll bleed to death." She studied me with intense concern, allowing her hands to be zip-tied.

Em Ho snorted at her, then looked at Shocker and bared his teeth. Last time he saw her she was wearing a skin-tight dress and brass knuckles. He rubbed the back of his head. Nodded to her and shrugged. "You extended that courtesy to me, so I will do the same." He snapped his fingers, pointed at my leg. "He hasn't suffered enough yet, anyhow."

One of the goons behind Diep put his gun in his waist and took several zip-ties from a pocket. He connected three of them end-to-end and wrapped it around my leg above the calf. I held my breath through the pain as he tightened it over the top of my blood soaked pants. He got blood on his thumb, made a face of disgust, wiped it off on my shirt. I wanted to hit him so terribly bad. He stood and resumed his place behind his boss. The pulse in my wound began to beat in my ears, *bump, bump-bump, you-need, drugs-now.*

I brightened momentarily. I still have some cocaine. I don't have to put up with this pain nonsense. I can snort it into oblivion. Hell, a bullet wound might even feel *good* after a dozen or so lines.

Getting ahead of yourself; you can't get to it with your hands tied and guns pointed at you, my subconscious pointed out. *Genius. What are you going to do, call time out for refreshments?*

"*Fuck you,*" I said.

Diep gave a narcotic grin and told me, "We have a lot to learn about each other, though we won't do it amorously."

"Amorously? Did you just call me gay?" I wheezed through gritted teeth. It was becoming a chore to keep focused on him.

"I was trying to be clever, based on your vulgar comment. But I see you aren't in a mood for cleverness. So let me be more direct. If anyone is fucked, it's you."

"How about sharing those Loratab's first?" I retorted. "I know you have some." He frowned, glanced at his cast. "If I'm going to be gayed upon, I need to be really hammered. Preferably ODed."

"Ha. I like you, Razor."

"Yeah, uh, my Gaydar told me that already." My jaw muscles ached, on the verge of locking up. I felt very dehydrated. It was unbelievably hard to keep up the dialogue, but I couldn't let myself go down without talking shit first.

Diep took his glasses off and pocketed them, eyes narrowed to wide slits. I had touched a nerve. He stepped toward me swiftly and planted his left foot, plunging forward with his right, soccer kicking my injured calf. BAM! The blow knocked me onto my side, legs jerking around awkwardly. With my arms restrained behind me I couldn't catch myself. Being in such a demeaning position in front of my crew pissed me off more than being shot did. I held in a monstrous roar of pain and rage, jaw burning well beyond the realm of normality.

"You would kick a man who's been shot and tied up," Bobby's deep voice boomed in anger. I struggled to a sitting position, looked over at Big Swoll, who seemed bigger and more swollen through my distorted sight.

"Be patient, whoever you are, black man," Diep told him, a slight slur hindering his words. "You'll get your turn." He snapped his fingers, pointed at the drone shed. "Put them in there. Bring Vietech."

Phong shouted orders in Vietnamese, and his subordinates carried me and herded my crew into the shed while he shouted more orders into his phone. The two gangsters toting me dumped me on the floor, pushed the others in. Blondie knelt over me and glared at them. The youngest gangster, who looked to be the brightest, did a thorough search through the desk, turned and looked at the books and manuals on the shelves, looking for tools we could use to escape with. The shed locked from the outside. All the tools were in the lab. We're screwed.

Maybe not ... my inner MacGyver whispered.

The thugs exited. The shed door rolled down, the latches were secured on the bottom of each side, *scrape-clank, scrape-clank.* It was dark without power, our eyes adjusting to the ambient glow coming under the door. Shocker, Ace and Bobby stood looking at the door. Shocker told Bobby, "Get our hands loose."

"Boss," he nodded to her. He bared his teeth, leaned over and *flexed.* The plastic zip-tie was strong and impossible for most humans to break. Bobby must have exerted several hundred pounds of pressure on it, a feat two of me couldn't do. He gave a loud grunt of satisfaction when it snapped, huge arms suddenly exploding out to his sides. Ace yelped as Bobby's fist struck him in the arm, knocking him into the steel wall.

Shocker turned her back to him. Blondie and I watched in amazement as he worked his over-developed fingers between her wrists, got a firm hold on the plastic and barked a burst of exertion, arms twitching quickly, breaking the tie with a loud *pop!*

Note to self: never, EVER, fuck with Bobby. The memory of Big Swoll throwing that scrub through the restaurant window came to mind and I laughed, gaining a few looks that suspected I was delirious.

Big Swoll broke mine next. The jolt made me see flashes of light in the black mist that swamped my peripheral senses. I leaned against the desk. Closed my eyes for a moment. Blondie, arms free, clenched her hands in angry indecision. I helped her out. "Babe, get my Go Juice."

She took a breath, visibly focusing, squatted down beside me, dug her little hand in my front pocket.

Undaunted by the fiery pain two feet below him, my Johnson thought about wriggling closer to her seeking fingers. I shook my head. There is something inherently wrong with me.

Her arousing search yielded a condom and a small Ziploc with approximately an eighth-of-an-ounce of cocaine in it. An "8 Ball" to all you former or current speed enthusiasts reading this. My girl's fingers quivered as she opened it, her eyes puffy and nose pink from emotion. She dipped a nail into the baggie, then held a mound of lovely white poison under my nose. I exhaled, leaned over and snorted it in one wop, groaning, tilting my head back. Shocker gave me a "Pfff" while the geek and Bobby looked on hopefully.

The drug melted, liquefying in my sinuses, absorbing, cruising past the blood-brain barrier in seconds. The numbing-zip took over and decided I didn't need neural pathways that reported pain: All nerves will hereby be commandeered under the Feel Good Act. Bullet wound? "Pfff," I said to that and the girl-beast who frowned disapproval at my first-aid solution. I took the Ziploc from Blondie and unloaded several more enormous bumps, eyeing Shocker challengingly. She folded her wings down sharply

A surge of energy flooded my limbs. I had enough presence of mind to know it was transient, and I needed to hurry and engineer a way out of this before my body bucked the Feel Good Act. My vision steadied, the shed and everything in it becoming more defined, and with it a plan began to stir in the part of my mind that stays on scheming stand-by regardless of my health. "I have an idea," I said, feeling in control once more.

Shocker took a roll of paper towels and a roll of duct tape from a shelf behind her, handed them to Blondie, who rolled up my pants leg and began constructing a compress.

She tore a strip of tape, affixed it over a folded wad of Brawny and said, "What's the plan, Babe?" She taped the bandage over my shin, then made another one for my calf before wrapping tape around my leg several times, finally stopping the bleeding.

I looked at my crew one at a time. Shocker had a wide range of emotions coursing through her entire body, as if several personalities were in there arguing about who should take the wheel for this situation. She was highly offended, and eager to do something about it. Ace wore a similar, though less aggressive, look of determination on his triangular jaw. Bobby looked puzzled, likely pondering how he came to be here with us crazy white motherfuckers, in this conundrum. Blondie sat on her heels, hands on my leg, looking into my eyes. She had shrugged off the panic, though I could tell a substantial amount of rage was suppressed between her boobies somewhere, energy she'll release on our foes at a more opportune time.

Aberrant feelings washed over my chest, killing my high. I wanted to embrace the bonding sensation, but it just wasn't one of my instincts. I was confused. I felt like these people were my family now. And it made me highly uncomfortable. *And pissed off*, I growled in thought, remembering the men outside. They have hurt countless people for no real reason or profit, and now my squad was on their radar. *Heh. Gaydar. I called Diep a fag ...* I shook my head, then snorted a magnificent drip. Ziiinggg! The bell tolled pleasure this time.

Now to business.

"Diep ordered Vietech to come up here. That means what?" I asked the two computer whizzes.

Ace answered. "He's going to find my computer in your lab. We had just set it up."

Blondie looked at him and smiled, her optimism fully restored. "I seriously doubt he could break into the

Wrecker."

Ace squinted a half smile. "No way."

"What about your rig?" I asked my girl, though I knew she never kept anything vital in it. My eyes couldn't help drifting to a spot between her legs.

She pouted her lips. "He could steal my e-book collection."

Ace laughed. He gave Blondie a smug look that said, *We're the shit, and everyone else just sucks.*

She smiled, *Mmm-hmm.*

"Razor!" Shocker barked at me. My indignant look just made her put her very capable hands on her hips. "Stop thinking about Blondie's hoo-hah and tell us the idea."

"Sorry. Got distracted. I'm delirious from the bullet wound." My sincere tone didn't seem to convince her. She didn't believe a word I said, but my effort made her see that I'm still in this and fit to lead.

"Coke-induced ADD is more like it," she said, relaxing her hands by her sides.

Blondie did a cute, miffed snort, and looked at me and Shocker like, *So you consider bullet wounds and cocaine as the reason he's unfocused, but not my hoo-hah???*

Maybe I read her expression wrong. She grabbed me to help me stand. I held my breath, ignored the cool, tingly-numb fire that stoked the lower portion of my leg and climbed to my feet. Held her and the desk for balance. Let go and waited for my head to stop spinning before I spoke. The sudden reset of equilibrium was refreshing.

I sighed. "Now. Back up to altitude. Let's assess our escape possibilities." I stretched my arms then spoke without looking directly at anyone, eyes darting around the shed. I pointed at the speakers on the shelf behind the desk, eight inch sub woofers in black boxes with mids and highs for full-range sound. They were expensive, and it stressed me to think about what we had to do to them. I said in a low voice, "We'll use the magnets on those Kenwoods to slide the latches open. A distraction will hold their attention so we can get out the door and disarm them. We'll need their guns to run off the rest."

"Um, question," Shocker said. "All that sounds spiffy. They certainly won't expect any coordinated attack. But how are we going to distract them from here?"

"We're not."

"Um..."

I looked at my girl. She read my thoughts and squealed, wagging her shoulders. "Babe! I've wanted to do this forever!" She patted her pockets and looked around in a half circle before remembering our phones had been taken, just as I did. "Shit," we said in unison.

Shocker's eyes widened in comprehension. "You can scald them!"

"With the little helicopters from Blondie's," Bobby said, chest muscles jumping energetically.

"Will they fly from Biloxi to Pass Christian?" Ace queried my girl.

She waved a dainty gesture. "Won't have to. I opened a Blondie's here last summer. The problem is, we don't have a phone."

My mind rushed with a solution. "You old Droid Razr is in the desk," I told her. The gangster missed it in his search.

She pouted again, this one making my optimism waiver. She glanced at Shocker dubiously, then told me, "I thought about that. It doesn't work."

I didn't recall her breaking it. "Huh?"

"I used the battery for something..."

I remembered. "Seymour. Bitch."

I sighed. Seymour was her vibrator. I supposed I shouldn't feel so annoyed, considering all the times I've witnessed her masterful skill with the toy. But I couldn't help it; Seymour's battery upgrade ruined my plan to get us out of here (And, if I'm to be honest, I had an irrepressible fear of the damned thing, ever since she threatened to work me over with it. I no longer allow her to bound and gag me).

Shocker seemed to ascertain that "Seymour" plus a cell phone battery plus me and Blondie equaled something sexual. She puffed her lips in derision, then wagged her ponytail and grinned. Ace shot her an embarrassed glance. Bobby stared at the door.

Why does it feel like my life has become a mash-up of *Sons of Anarchy* and *The Bold and the Beautiful?*

I restrained myself from screaming. My drugged mind realized I had seriously digressed as I rubbed my itchy, dehydrated eyes. "Coke-induced ADD," I mumbled, looking around. Shocker put her arms around Ace, hugged him briefly. Her compression sleeve shimmered like it was alive, a living organism with its own thoughts and drama, reflective scales on a body with superb power...

My eyes widened. I love it when a plan is just meant to be. I pointed at Shocker's magical arm and proclaimed grandly, "POWER."

Everyone looked from me to her. Ace grinned like a kid finding a Cracker Jack prize. He said, "Duh. We can power the phone with the Power Felt!"

"Shh," Shocker told him, looking at the door. "Not so loud." She was all teeth, though. "Should I warm it up?"

Ace's face scrunched in calculation. "Uh, she'll need to stream live video, which will require the full three-point-seven volts. So yeah. Warm it up, dear."

The girl-beast's shoulders relaxed, her feet widened, hands came up in loose fists, and she flowed smoothly into light-intensity shadowboxing, ducking, weaving, stepping around the drone throwing punches.

Blondie dug the phone out of the desk, stilettos tapping vibrations that my over-sensitive nerves rather enjoyed. She vibrated around me, returning to my side, seductive perfume tantalizing, testing my focus. I looked at her boobies. Looked at the Droid Razr she was dismantling. The back of it came off, battery box empty, brass terminals shining in the dim light cast by the crack under the door. I left the work up to them, watching as Big Swoll grabbed the two speakers off the shelf behind the desk. He lay them on the concrete, on their sides. He stood up straight, face showing reluctance for the chore. Raised his size 14 work boot. We both winced as he stomped the first one, composite box bursting like a Jack o'Lantern vandalized by mischievous trick-or-treater's.

Man, from now on we're keeping a tool set in here. Then, *Damn, I hope they don't come see what that noise was ...*

With both boxes open, Bobby and Ace removed the sub woofers, jagged fiberboard shards sticking out from them. Ace removed a length of speaker wire, handed it to Blondie. "That'll do it," she said. Her deft little fingers proceeded to connect it to the positive and negative terminals on the phone. Bobby put the speakers by the door and walked over to watch my girl work her engineering magic.

"Let's try it," Ace told Shocker.

She stopped, wiped thick sweat from her forehead. The shed was stifling in this heat without the door open. Ace unplugged a wire that connected her sleeve to the Power Felt tank top. Blondie handed him the wire that was connected to the phone. He squinted at it, pinching individual copper strands, separating them from where they stuck out of the clear, 16-gauge insulation. He twisted a few strands together on the positive side, a few on the negative, unable to use the entire wire; it was far too thick. With hands that worked the hair-thin strands with practiced ease, he slid the downsized wire into the output plug on Shocker's sweaty tank.

"We're in business," Blondie said as the Droid's screen

lit up in her hands, LCD bathing her face and boobies in bright white. The phone booted up. We waited impatiently.

"I want to see the photo," Bobby teased my girl.

"What?" she said. "My fuck-up?" He nodded. She cut her eyes at him. "It was an epic sunset, okay? It needed to be shared."

"So share," he replied, teeth bright in the dimness.

She snorted, *Forget you dude,* then looked at me, eyes searching mine. She leaned into me, kissed me slowly. "I'm sorry, Babe. No more Facebook. I promise."

I just looked at her. She wasn't getting off that easily. My non-response reiterated the I'll-deal-with-you-later promise. She accepted that with only a slight distasteful twist to her luscious lips. She looked at the phone, used the touchscreen to select the dial pad. Punched in a number and put it on speaker. It rang six times.

"*Hello*?" a girl answered in an irritated, you-freaking-woke-me voice.

Ms. All Business Blondie: "Diana! Get your ass up. You have work to do."

"Uh. Ma'am?" Diana quickly lost the attitude. I smiled at that. Sniffed a drip.

"I need you to go to the boutique and prepare a dozen coffees for Draganfly delivery."

"Uh..."

"You'll be paid for overtime."

"Double overtime," I added.

Blondie nodded. "I'll take care of you. Just hurry."

"O-kay," Diana said slowly. "You guys having a party or something?"

"Or something. How fast can you be there?"

"Um. Maybe twenty minutes?" Covers rustled in the background. I couldn't help picturing the blonde nineteen year old knockout climbing out of bed in a tee shirt and panties. I sniffed again, eyes darting.

"Make it ten," Blondie commanded her employee, "Skip the primp. This is an emergency."

"Yes, Ma'am."

"Call me as soon as you get there."

"Okay. I'll call you back."

Blondie ended the call. Shocker looked at her and commented, "I had my employees call me Boss or Clarice. Ma'am made me feel old."

Blondie shrugged. "Ma'am makes me feel like a madam."

Shocker was titillated. She gestured at me. "I thought he was the hooker boss."

"Oh, I am," I assured her, then pointed at the girls. "And I have two of the best hookers to ever bounce their boobies on these streets."

Blondie swatted my head. Shocker's eyes narrowed, but she couldn't make herself quit smiling. Ace and Bobby chuckled. Isn't it great that we can find humor at times like this?

Ain't nobody fresher than my motherfuckin' clique, clique, clique, my subconscious rapped.

I looked over at Big Swoll, realizing I knew absolutely nothing about him. I asked, "So what's your story? I know a little about the fugitives though nothing about you." I chuckled, "Well, except that you can Hulk-smash gangsters as well as you can speaker boxes."

He glanced at Shocker. Intertwined his hands in front of him, widened his stance. "Not much to tell, really. I'm married to a wonderful woman. We have six daughters." Ace's eyes widened at the "wonderful" description of Bobby's wife. Big Swoll shrugged. "I used to work for Clarice doing paint and body work. Now I do it for myself. And I'm presently training for an amateur bodybuilding competition."

That explains why he calls her boss ... I nodded

thoughtfully. Looked at his vascular arms. "Awesome. We'll go to your show." For some reason I felt compelled to shake his hand. I did so, Blondie frowning at me; I *never* shake hands. I said, "Pleasure to work with you."

"You too." His grin shined from his dark face.

I shook Ace's hand. Shocker's. Put a hand on my girl's shoulder. "We'll get out of this," I told my crew, deadly serious, "and we'll finish the job."

Everyone watched me. I looked each of them in the eye, knowing I was part of something truly special. These people were fighting for a good cause, with no percentage for themselves. And the best part?

They were *criminals!*

"Bitch."

Diana made it to the boutique in eleven minutes. She called Blondie. "The machines are on. The water will be hot in a few minutes," she reported. I pictured her behind the coffee bar, large stainless steel machines humming, heating the water that would become our weapon.

"Boil it. Hotter than usual. And I don't care what kind of coffee you make. Just put lots of chocolate and cream."

"Yeah. That'll stick to 'em," Bobby said.

"Stick to them?" Diana said, confused.

"Never mind," Blondie told her, frowning at Bobby. He mimed zipping his lips. "Get us six Draganflies ready for delivery."

"Yes, ma'am."

We waited perhaps another ten minutes - Diana was moving quickly, eager to impress for that double overtime payment-before the coffee was ready to fly. Blondie logged on to her store's website, entered her password and was able to selectively view what each helicopter saw, and even take over flight controls if she wanted. Master of flying puppets. "Oh yeah. We're gonna buzz them up," she told her Draganflies. Looked at me.

I said, "Get one overhead so we can figure out what Diep is doing. He's not going to just leave us in here. Hide the other five close by until we need them. We'll recon first, then decide how to hit them."

"Gotcha." She thumbed the screen, selecting a function on the site that allowed her to talk to her employees while piloting. She rang Diana's cell.

"Ma'am?"

"I need your help, um, delivering these."

"O-kay..." She paused in bafflement. Said, "I thought I was sending them to you."

"You are. Kind of." Blondie took a breath, glanced at everyone. There was a chance this girl would freak and call the cops. Shocker and Ace, being on the FBI's Most Wanted list, certainly couldn't afford that. And Blondie and I would let ourselves get killed before dialing 911. She had to solicit Diana's help carefully. "Remember when I told you how we could drop coffee on people that screwed with us?"

She giggled. "How could I forget? I have, like, ten ex-boyfriends I'd like to do that to."

"Well, how do you feel about Asian gangsters?"

"Gangsters? You're serious?"

"She's serious, Diana," I chimed in. "Just pretend you're playing *Angry Birds.*"

Ace snickered, "Angry Draganflies."

Bobby and Shocker looked at him in amazement, impressed. Apparently, he didn't crack many jokes.

Blondie, mouth parted, like we were stealing her role in the show, thrust out a hip, planted an exasperated hand on it and reprimanded us, "Excuse me."

"*Mea culpa*, Babe." I gestured, *Please go on.* Everyone paid attention once more.

She told her employee, "Yes, I'm serious. I need you to help us out of a bad situation. You can fly better than anyone else. We'll hold up for any trouble with the cops," she added hastily, as Diana started to protest. "I know you aren't the bad girl type. This really isn't against the law. It's self-defense."

"We're helping law enforcement," I added, making Shocker giggle-snort, embarrassing herself.

"Helping law enforcement," Diana said cynically. I pictured her with a reluctant pout. She sighed as if knowing she would regret this. Then gave in. "So these gangsters are there now?"

~ ~ ~

Diana landed five Draganflies on the south side of the condo building's roof, hiding them from our enemies while making them quickly accessible. Blondie controlled #6, hovering it fifty feet above the garage while Shocker shadowboxed to keep the phone juiced up.

I looked at the Droid screen. The Dragonfly's camera showed the top of the garage: two sheds, the El Camino, Ford, and my Suzuki, all itty-bitty looking. The condo's roof behind us, a highway of headlights out front. Street lights everywhere. Blondie zoomed in on our shed. Two Viet guards stood outside the door, fifteen feet away, near the edge. She turned the camera on the lab. The door was open, a light on inside. *Yeah, they brought a power source. A battery and a power inverter. Or a fuel cell. I would have heard a generator...*

Blondie flew closer and zoomed inside. Several steel tables were positioned around the walls of the lab, loaded with tools and various equipment in neat rows, more on shelves above the tables. Consumables and other supplies underneath on the floor. On a workbench to the left was an enormous black computer, Ace's Wrecker, with an Asian kid sitting in front of it.

"Vietech," Blondie growled.

"*That's* him?" Shocker said from the other side of Blondie. "He looks like he's twelve."

"I don't know how old he is. Gotta be at least twenty-five," Blondie said.

Ace moved his girl aside and squinted at the screen. "T'heh. He can't even get past the screensaver."

Blondie smirked at him, but lost her spirit when she looked back at the phone. "Uh-oh. What's this?"

I looked closely. Several well-dressed thugs walked out onto the roof and headed for our prison. I said, "If they come in just put your hands behind your back. Follow my lead." Everyone whispered or nodded agreement.

We watched as they stopped outside and attached something next to the door, about shoulder high. Blondie zoomed in on it. The device was the size of a Big Mac, squarish, dark colored with several wires and two red LEDs. I sighed. "Diep has the good stuff. This isn't fun anymore."

Ace peered at the Droid closely. "That's an explosive with a remote detonator," he said, just reporting the facts. "An old Claymore."

Shocker stopped shadowboxing and gave him a terrified stare. The geek in him withered and the husband-father surfaced. Panic pulsed from him as he stepped to his wife and hugged her, the stress infecting Bobby, then us. I couldn't imagine what was going through their heads. They had kids. Families. Blondie just looked pissed. I had no opinion yet, likely due to the shock of the wound and the fantastic drug dampening my emotions.

Which reminds me ...

I sat on the desk. Took my Ziploc out and snorted a large dose up each nostril. "Aaaahh! Better." I put it away. Wiped my nostrils, fingers. Smiled hugely at my squad. "Shall we expedite our exit?"

The girl-beast clenched her fists in front of her, frustrated at me, them, the world. "You goddamn lunatic," she told me. She pointed at the door. "There's a bomb about to turn us into air pollution and you're getting high?!"

"I'm not getting high." I scowled defensively. "I was already high."

Did her eyes just flash red? I looked at the phone. Blondie worked the helicopter's camera so we could see the thugs walk into the lab and gesture at Vietech to hurry up. The hacker didn't even turn to look at them, completely absorbed with breaking into Ace's monstrous computer, eyes locked on the over-sized screen in front of him. I could just barely make out that he was typing furiously on the keyboard. She spun the camera back to our shed. The thugs set to guard us were glancing at the bomb and muttering to each other, fingering the guns in their waistbands nervously.

I put a hand on my girl's shoulder. "Have Diana position the other Draganflies over the lab. Tell her to scald them as soon as they come out, then unload the pepper spray. On my signal scald the two outside the door. When we get out put that bomb on a flight into the ocean."

"Gotcha Raz." Her eyes narrowed. She started to call Diana.

"Wait. Wait Wait Wait," I said, eyes closed. I shook my head as if I had left out something vital. Looked at her. "We need some music."

She smiled agreement.

Shocker snorted, then said, "You are unbelievable."

"I know." I shot imaginary cuffs, smoothed my hair back.

"What are you in the mood for? Pantera?" Blondie asked.

I looked around, tapping a finger to my lips. Got it! *"Man in the Box* by Alice in Chains."

"Alice who?" Bobby said.

Blondie chortled, called Diana. Shocker seemed to reconsider her ridicule after hearing my song choice. Hey, the music should fit the setting, right? I saw no reason we shouldn't do this with style.

I nodded to the girl-beast. "Just do your thing. Take them out." She grunted. I said to Ace, "Uh, don't get in the way. Bobby, grab a speaker."

I limped over to the door and picked up a sub-woofer. Big Swoll grabbed the other. We squatted down by the sides, him on the left, me on the right, and stuck the magnets to the steel, on the very bottom where the sliding locks were. I looked at my girl. She nodded, *Ready*. I grinned at her and said, "Let's jam."

Two second later, through the thin steel door we heard heavy metal guitar chords precede faint splashes and two loud yelps. We dragged the speakers across the metal quickly. The locks freed, the door popped open slightly. Yanking the speakers off, we pushed the door up and charged out.

Bobby, with two good legs, made it to our guards first. He rammed into them as they grabbed for their guns, knocking one on his back. I jumped on top of the fallen gangster and introduced him to my fist. Repeatedly. Then I flipped him over and took my razor from his pocket. Indescribable relief flooded me as I palmed the handle, sheathed it. I told the unconscious man, "Thanks for holding that for me."

The other guard had been standing near the edge of the roof when Bobby hit him. The blow had so much force the guy flew over the side, and would have dropped six stories if Bobby hadn't reached out and snatched him back. The gangster's face showed relief a microsecond before Bobby smashed it into oblivion with a huge elbow.

Splashes and shouts alerted us to the goons coming out of the lab. Shocker was already on them, fists of fury bashing into their scalded, pepper-sprayed bodies. Four Draganflies buzzed over the fight. "I'm the man in the box!" their tiny speakers wailed, surprisingly loud, spurring

Shocker's performance.

Blondie had dropped the phone and grabbed the explosive. A Draganfly descended, expertly piloted by Diana, and Blondie dropped the bomb into its cargo box. It hummed away quickly, disappearing in the direction of the Gulf. Blondie didn't waste time watching it, trusting Diana to handle up. She ran over to aid Shocker, yanking a gun out of an enemy's hand right as he aimed it at the fierce legend. The pistol popped a tongue of fire into the night sky, and seconds later a Draganfly crashed into Blondie's truck. She saw her paint job ruined, shrieked in rage, and wopped her target in the head with his own weapon. Turned and pointed it at the thug still standing. He held his hands up. Shocker turned from the two she had taken out, walked over to him almost nonchalantly and drilled him with a lead-right. His attempt to block her punch was comical. He joined his pals on the concrete.

"Hell yeah!" I resisted the urge to jam my air guitar, limped over to the lab. Ignored the frightened Viet geek that babbled incoherent pleas while I searched for his power source. "Where is it?" I shouted at Vietech.

"W-what?" His glasses looked as fragile as his tiny frame, sharp cheekbones and pathetic chin just begging for my fist.

"The cell." I traced the computer's power cord with my eyes.

"I—"

Crack! I slapped him. "Never mind. I found it."

Blondie came in behind me and pistol whipped her squealing rival to sleep while I unplugged the lamp and computer from the power cell. Bobby saw I was struggling to carry it and took it from me. Damn thing wasn't all that heavy – it was about the size of a large couch cushion, maybe forty pounds, metal frame with several deep cycle batteries in it. But my leg wasn't going for it, numbly-drugged or not.

"Where?" Bobby said.

"Outside. Breaker box by the entrance."

He ran out. I looked around and grabbed some wire from under a bench, hurried after him. Diep's people had cut the power at the main breakers on the ground level. And we needed to get the vault door closed before they responded to that gunshot. The power cell was the only source that could do it.

Shocker paced back and forth in front of her victims, veins bulging all over, snarling in her lovely demonic way, looking like she hoped one of them would wake up so she could put them back to sleep. I nodded to her, limp-running over to the breaker box. Bobby, kneeling next to the open vault door, adjusted the dials on the power cell's digital readout. I stumbled down next to him and opened the panel in the concrete next to the door, ran a finger down the breakers, stopping on the one we needed.

"They're coming," Blondie reported, looking through the entrance, down the ramp. Racing engines and squealing tires from multiple vehicles echoed up the levels. We had to get the door closed fast.

I popped out the breaker. Palmed it and looked at the wire in my other hand. It was a length of extension cord, minus the plugs on the ends, white, green and black wires encased in orange insulation. They were already stripped, thankfully. I pressed the white wire into the breaker slot and forced the breaker back into its place over it, having to push hard enough to make me see stars. Dizzy, I turned to the power cell. Like a generator it had multiple outlets. I chose the one for 240 volt appliances, quickly sliding the white wire in the short slot and the black wire in the tall slot.

"Got it?" Blondie asked from the far side of the entrance, hand poised in front of the keypad. The sounds of Diep's death squad just underneath us and approaching fast made her eyes dance with apprehension.

I nodded to her, stood like a drunk and turned back to the breaker box. I grabbed the black wire and touched it to the metal housing in the panel, grounding the circuit. The keypad lit up, and the motor for the door had power. Blondie typed frantically. I let out a breath when the door began cycling closed.

Exhaust pipes from highly revved Honda's bellowed up the ramp from the fifth to the sixth level. A yellow Accord was the first one visible, a train of multicolored, customized Toyota's and Acura's tight behind it. The driver of the Accord saw the vault door sliding closed and gunned it. The door was nearly shut when he rammed into it. The booming destruction of his car shook the building. Blondie screamed as plastic and glass projectiles flew through the opening and lacerated her upraised arms, a chunk of yellow bumper cutting her forearm badly.

The door crushed the car's bumper, grill and hood like a trash compactor before stuttering to a halt. The gap was big enough for a person to slip through. I had no plans to hold them off with the few guns we had taken; our ammo would run out before theirs. We needed to get off this roof.

I grabbed Blondie's shoulders, searching her for debilitating inquiries. "You okay?"

"Yeah." She clenched her bleeding forearm, looking at the still-open door. "They'll come through in a minute. Are we going down the rope?"

"Only way. Give me a gun." She handed me a black .380 Beretta. I kissed her and gave an encouraging smile. "Get them down to the street. Rendezvous B."

"All right. Hurry."

She jogged over to the edge of the roof facing the condos and picked up a black garbage bag. Opened it and pulled out the one hundred foot rope inside. She made sure one end was still securely tied to its anchor and threw it over. She told everyone to follow and went down first, blonde hair flying haphazardly.

Shocker gave me a concerned look. I waved for her to go down and stuck the Beretta through the door, squeezed off a couple of shots. I couldn't see where my targets were, but they immediately returned fire, bullets from pistols and semi-auto rifles pinging into the thick steel I put my back against, a few zipping through the gap, heading straight into the condos. *At least no one lives there yet*, I thought, wincing at the concussive vibrations ringing from the door.

As soon as their shooting lulled I turned and fired through the opening again, hoping the gun had a full clip. Glanced at my crew. Blondie, Ace, and Bobby had gone down, Shocker just stepping over the edge. As soon as she slid down I would run over and rapell down before anyone came through and saw how we escaped.

I could hear Diep barking orders to Phong, who shouted rapid, harsh Vietnamese to his soldiers. Suddenly, a fusillade of bullets tore into the door, ricocheting dangerously off the car and concrete. They were trying to hit me with a rebound. I glanced at the rope, judging Shocker to have descended most of the way by now. The concentrated fire stopped, the men reloading, and I fired at them again, the pops minuscule after the impressive assault. When they opened fire again, I dropped the spent Beretta and ran for the rope.

The fifty feet to my exit was too much for my leg. The damn thing decided that *now* was the perfect time to refuse to work. I tripped over my own feet, chest and elbows taking the impact, tiny rocks breaking skin. I choked out, "*Fuck* that hurt." Pain lanced through my entire body. The black mist returned, and I had no control for a moment. I rode it out, vision clearing somewhat. I regained full consciousness, realized what had happened and turned to look at the entrance right as several gangsters sprang off the Accord's crumpled front end, through the gap, MAK 90s in their hands.

I turned over and did my best to crawl-walk to the rope, the anchor and knot still over thirty feet away. I wasn't going to make it. *"Let's go after the Tiger Society,"* I said in falsetto, mimicking myself. *"Let's make things RIGHT."* I sighed a growl. "You suck, Eddy."

I decided I wasn't going out like a trampled, crawling mutt. I stood and faced the men I knew would empty their 30-round clips into my body. Four were through and had their assault rifles directed right at me, walking with hatred wrinkling their faces. I snorted my final, lovely drip. Smacked my lips in pleasure, then told them, "Kiss my ass."

I would have mooned them if I didn't think I would fall on my face.

They didn't immediately shoot, knowing they had me. They spread out, crouched and scanned the roof like they knew what they were doing, lifted their weapons to their shoulders to waste me. Triumphant smiles stretched their cheeks, fingers tightening on triggers, expressions abruptly turning startled as they were knocked off their feet in quick succession. The silent sniper fire whizzed by from behind me. *Thud-thud-thud-thud,* they went down like video game targets.

I wheezed out a laugh. Spun around. On the roof of the condos was a figure in black, a familiar tripod mounted rifle in front of him. "Loc," I muttered. Then got mad. I shook both fists at him, pointed at my leg. *"Now* you help?! You're a little late!"

Did he shrug? With the relief of not being dead came the inspiration to dig deep and push myself into a limping trot for the rope. I heard two more men cry out as they came through the gap and took rounds from our crew's mysterious sniper. I slid down entirely too fast, weak arms unable to make my hands grip the nylon, palms burning severely. I made it about four levels down before blacking out and falling into pain-free nothingness.

❋ ❋ ❋

Thank you for reading.
Please review this book. Reviews help others find New Pulp Press and inspire us to keep providing these marvelous tales.

If you would like to be put on our email list to receive updates on new releases, contests, and promotions, please go to NewPulpPress.com and sign up.

Acknowledgements

I began writing this the same month Dennis Newton and I published Shocking Circumstances, in September, 2012. It took sixteen months of rewriting these chapters by hand while Dennis patiently supplied my innumerable research requests to complete the manuscript. He was halfway through typing it when he died of a pulmonary embolism. We have published two novels (mine), a history (his), and two children's books (his text, my illustrations) together. I miss our team work. I miss him. His extraordinary charity work, especially those efforts that helped children and the poor, lives on. Dennis, I hope one of our works will continue your legacy – this one's for you my friend!

The characters in this novel are from my previous books: Razor and Blondie in By Hook or Crook, and Shocker and her guys in Shocking Circumstances. The idea to cast these wildly different personalities into one storyline belongs to my Aunt Wendie. Teaming them up seemed incongruous, but the blend of personalities complemented each other. It drove me mad, but it worked. Thanks Nanny!

My very good friend and protégé, Thong 'Tony' Le, provided me with invaluable insight into Vietnamese culture, traditions, and language. This novel wouldn't exist without his perseverance and help. There are probably some inaccuracies, and certainly some exaggerations, all of which are my own. Tony, I value our friendship, and thank you for being a brother to me. I sincerely hope the Vietnamese Mafia doesn't scuff you for my portrayal of their lives. Du ma! It's HBL, always.

My mother, Troie Roy, suffered through the Herculean

task of reading my handwritten chapters, and provided me use of her clever mind. Mom, the suggestions you noted were just what I needed. I used all of them! Thanks for being so awesome.

Marina Stone is a real Gem. She took the time to help her obnoxious bro resolve a major problem with the publisher. Thanks for the help, my dear evil genius of a sister.

Fred Williams taught me boxing and has been a great mentor and friend for half my life. The boxing described in my stories is accurate, and hopefully entertaining, because of the discipline Fred instilled in me. Fred is one of the best pugilist coaches ever, a master of motivating people, and I can only hope the guys I train respect me half as much as countless boxers respect Fred. Old Man, I love you and appreciate you.

Friend and fellow outlaw, Roy Harper, has heard every story idea I've ever considered since I began penning novels. His blunt feedback was essential to keeping my farfetched ideas off paper, and his perpetual skepticism has always balanced out my overly optimistic views of reality. Together we started Criminal Ventures Books, and hope to grow it into a profitable enterprise as we continue adding more books to our catalog. Roy, buena suerte with your new publisher, Crime Wave Press. I look forward to working with you guys to sell the Tool's Law series. And thanks for the life insurance!

I have to mention my friends and test readers that were vital to keeping me motivated on this project: Barry Ellender and David Bass. My guys, if I get rich on this one, you already know what's going down ...

And I couldn't possibly leave out my woman, Melanie Jean, whose warm heart has thawed mine, and who was considerate enough to help in the final formatting of this. Babe, I look forward to partnering with you, warriors in The

Battle of Queries, kicking down publisher's doors and challenging them to sell crime fiction by real criminals!

I love all of you wonderful MFers.

Chris Roy
Parchman, Mississippi
July, 2015

About the Author

Chris Roy was born and raised on the Mississippi Gulf Coast. He has a background in automotive mechanics, tattoo art, and pursues many passions, including boxing and fitness training.

Chris currently resides at the Mississippi State Penitentiary in Parchman. If you would like to correspond with the author, you can send a letter to:

Chris Roy K8649
MSP Unit 29
PO Box 1057
Parchman, Ms. 38738

NewPulpPress.com